MURDER IN HAMPSTEAD

A classic whodunnit in a contemporary setting

SABINA MANEA

THE BOOK FOLKS

Published by

The Book Folks

London, 2021

This book is a work of fiction. Names, characters, businesses, organizations, places and events are either the product of the author's imagination or are used fictitiously. Any resemblance to actual persons, living or dead, events or locales is entirely coincidental. The spelling is British English.

ISBN 978-1-913516-17-8

www.thebookfolks.com

For the three Badgers: Edwin, Robin and Francis

Prologue

Friday, 4th September (the day of the murder)

The murder took place on a late afternoon in September.

Lucia stumbled in from an errand to find a small party in full swing. The French doors in the drawing room had been flung open, and a table heaving with high tea had been set on the mossy stone paving. Professor Alla Kiseleva held court in a flowing dress. Emilia Poole was in thrall to a sinewy, straight-backed man in his sixties. Adam Corcoran clutched a near-empty glass of champagne, his glassy gaze drifting off while a loud City type brayed on. The expensive-looking wife hovered expectantly, knowing she'd be ignored.

Mrs Byrne, brimming with nervous energy, sauntered over to Lucia. 'Oh, you're back, child. I forgot to tell you. The Professor fancied she'd have a gathering – what with the weather being so nice. She has these whims, you see, goes for weeks locked up with Emilia and her books, then decides to invite everyone round.'

It wasn't unexpected – once hired, tradespeople were generally forgotten about. The housekeeper nudged Lucia and whispered, 'At least it shows she's still human, eh?'

The Professor caught Lucia's eye. 'Come have some tea and meet everyone.' They all gathered around, gawping. 'This is Lucia Steer, our decorator – sorry, interior designer. She's doing a splendid job – Margaret wanted to know where you got the teal wallpaper in the hallway. My neighbours, Margaret and John Walker.'

The wife was thrilled at being noticed at last. 'It's gorgeous. And you're an interior designer! How lovely! We're looking to have the house done, aren't we, Johnny, and what's better than a personal recommendation, isn't that what you always say?'

Johnny looked unimpressed. Dealing with the staff was clearly not on his list of domestic duties. He took a step back, as if getting too close might dirty his beautifully cut suit, the pinstripes of which he'd regrettably got wrong – too wide for a barrister. 'Yes, well. Do you work with anyone else?'

Uncharacteristically, the question took Lucia by surprise. 'Yes, I have a couple of lads who help out.'

'You'd need more manpower to tackle our house.' They were back on familiar territory now.

'My clients prefer me to a load of boys drinking tea and playing with rollers. There's plenty of manpower available at the Red Lion down the hill, if that's what you're after.'

The tamed barrister grimaced and stared at the sandwiches. The Professor grinned appreciatively. She looked peaky. 'Let me introduce you to Dr Edmund Glover, my GP.' She beckoned to the elegant man in Emilia's company. 'And you know Emilia, of course. Dr Glover, this is Lucia. Don't make any jibes at her being a lady decorator unless you want to be eviscerated in public.'

'I wouldn't dream of being so tasteless.' Dr Glover smiled winningly, like a panther weighing up the merits of its prey. 'I think it's marvellous to have given up a desk job for something so enjoyably physical.' He waited to ascertain from her reaction how close to the mark he was.

Lucia returned a blank stare. 'How's the book going, Professor?'

The Professor sighed, relieved to be restored into focus. 'Good days and bad days. Do you know anything about cybernetics?'

'In the Soviet or the American sense?'

'Very good. Both, actually; rather, how Soviet research influenced the Americans. Emilia has been invaluable – organising my papers and transcribing my scribbles. Slowly, slowly, we're making progress.'

'It's fascinating,' Emilia joined in. 'I didn't know anything about cybernetics before I started working for the Professor. I just hope my proofreading is up to scratch.' She manifestly believed it was. Her lightly freckled face was almost bare, and she looked younger than her years. The plain summer dress added weight to the convincing picture of simplicity.

Adam, who had stationed himself within immediate reach of the champagne, trundled towards them. He had been abandoned by the Walkers, by now immersed in a quiet marital spat at the other end of the terrace. 'Lucia, how nice to see you. Aunt Alla, did I tell you she used to be a lawyer? She could help with selling the house – save us a few pennies and all that.' The alcohol had loosened his self-control. He looked defiant, like a wilful teenager pushing for a reaction.

The Professor was stony-faced. Dr Glover and Emilia visibly held their breath. Lucia broke the silence, 'I didn't know you were looking to sell.'

Adam pressed further, seeing that his target didn't take the bait. 'They'll take it off your hands in a second, Auntie, you know that. A lick of paint and you and Mrs B could be out of here and into a chic little cottage by the Heath.'

'We'll see. Early days yet.' The Professor had regained her composure and gave Adam a pitying look.

Mrs Byrne had crept upon the group and was fixated on Adam's glass. 'Do you want some tea, Adam?'

'No, Mrs B, it's too late for caffeine. More of that delightful fizz is what I want – while it's still flowing freely.' Having delivered the parting shot, he swung on his heels and headed back to the spread, blind to the housekeeper's reproachful gaze.

'You must excuse Adam. He has so many ideas about what's best for me. He gets ahead of himself sometimes.' The Professor wiped her brow. It wasn't sufficiently hot to be sweating. Her hand was shaking violently as she put her glass down on the table. Lucia had been so engrossed in the peculiarity of the occasion that she'd only just noticed the old-fashioned coupe with an exquisite fish scale pattern. Everyone else was drinking out of ordinary flutes.

'Excuse me, I feel a little off. Must be the sun. Mrs Byrne, could you fetch me some water, please?' The Professor stumbled and swayed her way down to the stone step. The lush garden stretched out before her, impassive to her predicament. Without warning, she started convulsing violently, her limbs twisted, her face frozen as neurotransmitters fed into her body the knowledge that there was no redemption. What was left of her lay on the ground, draped in the shell of her now purposeless clothes. Silence weighed down on the house, as if a film had been paused.

The first sound was an agonising scream from Margaret. Dr Glover, his training having kicked in, rushed over to administer first aid. A panoply of formulaic human responses followed – Margaret, Emilia and Mrs Byrne were crying at various volumes, while Adam and John Walker settled for mute distress and unmistakable nausea.

Lucia heard her own voice speaking to the 999 operator. The ambulance arrived a few minutes later, promptly dispatched from the Royal Free. The suddenness of the incident triggered the usual protocol of notifying the police. The place was soon teeming with uniforms.

Chapter 1

Friday, 21st August (two weeks before the murder)

The alarm rang and Lucia Steer willed herself out of bed, heavy with sleep. By the time she reached the bathroom mirror she was fully awake. She gave herself the usual morning appraisal – it was her ritual to set her up for the day ahead, to reassure her that whatever the challenges would be, she was ready to take them on. She was thirty-seven, with shoulder-length brown hair that changed subtly with the seasons, and slightly oversized features. The frank, expressive eyes were too large, the nose was too long, and the mouth was too big, as if they had been mismatched with the face. She had a knack for turning heads as she walked into a room, with her easy confidence that really got under your skin.

The flat she rented in Hampstead was in a dull red-brick block, furnished like a hotel except for the books that took up a whole wall in the bare living room. The contents of her wardrobe had been whittled down to a suitcase's worth, as if she had to pack and go at a moment's notice.

Lucia allowed her mind to wander. She didn't regret walking away from a legal career to strike out on her own as an interior designer. She could still conjure up the exhilaration of leaving the office for the last time that thick, close summer's evening three years previously. The following morning, she'd bought herself a white van. The salesman had weighed her up with amusement. It turned out she was serious, with her generous leaving bonus, so he sold her the best he had – a Transit Custom Sport with an extravagant body kit. At last, her life was finally about to begin.

Lucia scrolled quickly through her phone. She was planning to head out shopping for new supplies. Flicking through fabric swatches and drawing up mood boards was all very good, but she also liked the manual labour. Stripping and painting were satisfying and therapeutic, so unlike being chained to a desk poring over commercial documents.

She had her eye on a very big prize. Beatrice Hall, the local Victorian monstrosity, was legendary among North London builders. Rumours had been circulating of late that the owner, a reclusive Russian scientist whom nobody had ever met, was looking for decorators. A job that size would be the making of any tradesman, and Lucia knew she was up against Danny Garrett. With his boundless confidence, he was certain he would get it. He lorded over Hampstead in the knowledge that no self-respecting banker's wife would employ anyone else. After all, he was unparalleled at sweet-talking them into doing three times more work than they had asked for. He also knew his coarse good looks were just the ticket to console them for their husbands' neglect.

Lucia had first crossed paths with Danny at the builders' merchant in Colindale, where she used to attract confused stares from the various muscled men who inhabited the shop floor. The idea that she was one of them had caused much amusement at first. A few had tried it on, of course, and were swatted off like flies. Those that patronized her – they couldn't imagine she knew anything about tools or painting – soon found out just how icy her stare was, how annihilating her put-downs, and quickly learned to behave. She gained their respect because she was so sure of herself, without scrimping or cutting corners or wasting time with empty talk. It was this attitude that brought in her first clients, and it kept them coming. Danny never did warm up to her. She was a threat, the probable end of his long reign of tea drinking and snail's pace work.

'Morning, Danny.' Lucia was determined to maintain a veneer of politeness, even though he made her skin crawl with his unpleasant gaze, a mixture of arrogance, lecherousness and contempt.

'Lucia.' This time he made a passable attempt at the Italian pronunciation, an outward sign of reluctant acceptance that she was a permanent fixture. 'Stocking up then? Did you hear Beatrice Hall is up for grabs?'

Lucia shot him a sideways glance, a preliminary warning shot. 'Yes, I'd heard something. Are you thinking of quoting for it then?'

'Quoting? You make me laugh. I know that young geezer the Professor's got in to clean up the place. Adam Corcoran, he's called. He's her nephew. When I bumped into him down the Red Lion the other day, he told me they're looking to have the whole pad done up, top to bottom. So yeah, I think I'm pretty much in there, y'know.'

Lucia smiled like a winsome Medusa. 'Well, Danny, I guess they'll have a choice then. I'm quoting for the Hall.'

'Suit yourself, Lucia. Think you're wasting your time though. This is a big job – a man's job, right, lads?' A couple of them laughed to keep up, so he knew they were on his side. They too weren't best pleased that Lucia had rocked up out of nowhere to steal their thunder.

'I was thinking I'd get a reference from the Leclercs. They were so chuffed with the way their house turned out. You remember them, don't you, Danny?'

Danny winced. He remembered the Leclercs better than he cared to admit. He'd got the gig after doing his usual magic trick on Madame Leclerc but got sloppy and fell foul of the husband. Monsieur Leclerc wasn't best pleased when he came home early one day and found his wife doing some serious damage to the new sofa with Danny. Mr Leclerc was a tall, wiry Swiss who spent a lot of time at the gym, so Danny got a punch on the nose and a kick up the backside, and no more work from them. Naturally, Lucia swooped in to pick up the pieces. The story had made the rounds in the Red Lion, and he didn't want to be reminded of it. Luckily the Leclercs had moved back home last month, so it was just starting to blow over.

'Danny, you legend, that was classic! Caught you with them all the way down, didn't he?'

Danny could have done without the sarcasm from his apprentice. Everyone knew Jimbo was always eyeing up some business on the side.

'Well, gents, have a good day. Danny, I'm sure I'll see you around.' Lucia walked out, conscious of all eyes resting on her.

Being the only woman in a man's world didn't bother her in the slightest. She found she tended to prefer it to female company. Men were simple creatures, motivated by a finite set of goals and with predictable reactions to a short list of stimuli. With women, she never knew where she stood, whether they genuinely wanted to be friends or were laughing at her behind her back.

Chapter 2

Friday, 28th to Saturday, 29th August (one week before the murder)

Lucia pushed open the pub door and was met with the overwhelming stench of Lynx. She knew most of them by now – young men in their twenties with fresh undercuts, tight T-shirts, and elaborate tattoo sleeves. They were harmless. Nobody else but the local builders and their occasional female hangers-on drank in the Red Lion. It was the stepping-stone for the usual Friday night carnage down in Camden. They were the ones lucky enough to afford this pastime – the rest had to make do with cans of weak lager on a bench before heading back to their dingy shared housing in East London.

'Usual?' The barmaid eyed up the unopened white Burgundy, which only Lucia and the landlady drank.

'Not today, thanks, Becky. Listen, do you know if a guy called Adam Corcoran comes here?'

'Yeah, I know Adam. Quiet guy. Doesn't really fit in with these lunatics. He's over there in the corner, by the window. Why do you ask?'

'I hear he's in charge of Beatrice Hall. I wouldn't mind that job if it's going.'

Becky raised a perfectly drawn eyebrow. 'Beatrice Hall? I heard Danny Garrett's after that.'

'I know. Which is why I'm after it too.'

'Suit yourself, babe, but I'd watch my back if I were you. You know how he holds a grudge.'

'I always do. I'll go have a word with this Adam bloke then. See you later, Becky.'

Lucia saw a washed-out man in his early thirties, feverishly tapping on his phone, half-drunk pint on the table. His cuticles were bleeding, and there were thin lines of sweat running down his temples. Accountant, or tax lawyer at a stretch. He had that air of commitment to an outwardly dull but inwardly all-consuming profession. He finally sensed her staring down at him and looked up.

'Hi. Are you alright?' His eyes flickered appreciatively. Her hair was still streaked with gold from the summer sun.

'Hi. You're Adam Corcoran, right?' He nodded and gestured to the free bench opposite him. 'My name's Lucia Steer. I hear you're after a decorator for Beatrice Hall. I'm interested in the job.'

'I like it, Lucia. Straight in there, no messing.'

He had a few inside him – not drunk, just merry and overly confident. Perfect state of mind.

'News travels fast around here then,' he said. 'The place hasn't been touched in years. I'm trying to convince Aunt Alla to smarten it up a bit. It's not like she can't afford it.' He laughed, somewhat bitterly. 'Tell you what. Why don't you come have a tour and see what you think?'

'Sounds good. I can do tomorrow, even though it's a Saturday, if that suits. Do you want me to bring references?'

'Don't worry, I'll do my own digging. I like to think I'm a good judge of people. Sorry to be boring, but I've got to make a move. Shall we say nine thirty?'

'Perfect. See you then. Good to meet you, Adam, and thanks again.'

He gobbled his drink with a trembling hand and got up to leave.

The day after, Lucia circled Beatrice Hall before ringing the bell at the outer gate. The building was a doll's house of Gothic Revival turrets and Italianate window arches. Close up, the bright red and yellow brick had dulled to a dirty brown, like everything in the city eventually did. It was the housekeeper who opened the door before handing her over to Adam. She introduced herself as Mrs Byrne – glum, bloodless, with a raspy Irish voice. Inside, the overload of porphyry and stained glass jarred, like a silent film set.

As anticipated, the house rested uneasily on its former glory. It had been reduced to a rabbit's warren of musty corridors and garishly wallpapered, mostly uninhabited rooms. Lucia had never taken on a job that size. 'It's a big project. We'll need to strip the walls and fix the plaster underneath before we can make a clean start. Hopefully, the plaster underneath is sound, and then my guy will only have to skim here and there. It'll take a month, if not longer. You're probably looking at ten to twelve grand, not including the new paint and wallpaper. I don't think any of the lot in here can do better than that.'

'I believe you, Lucia. I've talked it through with Aunt Alla, and she's given me free rein to get this place sorted. If you're sure you can do it, the job's yours. Can you start on Monday?'

'You're in luck. I've just wrapped up my last commission.'

They shook on it, and Lucia found herself yearning for fresh air. Outside, she stood on the pavement, triumphant. It had been peculiarly straightforward. On the other hand, tracking down decorators was a lot of effort, and having one offer their services must have been a godsend.

She was about to start her van when she heard her name from the other side of the street. Danny Garrett crossed slowly towards her, hatred and disbelief etched into his coarse face. She had taken too many jobs from under his nose to expect friendliness.

'You've been to the Hall then. What's up?' He wasn't one for manners or false politeness.

'I got the job.'

'What d'you mean, you got the job?'

'The painting job. Doing up the Hall. Adam's given it to me.'

Danny was visibly grinding his teeth. For a moment she was afraid he might hit her. She straightened her back and pulled herself together. She wasn't going to let a thug like him intimidate her. He backed off, annoyed that his aggression was bearing no fruit. 'So, you got one up on me, Lucia. I hope you've got the stomach for it, if you catch my drift.'

'I don't, and frankly I don't care, Danny. I beat you, and you don't like it. Live with it.'

'Well, don't kid yourself, sweetheart. I'm still the boss around here, remember.'

Lucia laughed and got behind the wheel. She knew she'd rattled him. This called for a celebration. She decided she would treat herself to a meal out – nothing special, just a bowl of noodles and a glass of wine at the Blue Fish.

The restaurant was empty, save for a man huddled at a table in the window, tapping anxiously with slightly yellowed fingers as he waited to be served. Early fifties, fair hair that had been spared the grey, a weathered face that could have been attractive. His shirt and trousers looked averse to the ironing board. Lucia watched him for a while as they ate their respective meals in silence. As she was getting ready to leave, an impulse got the better of her.

'Sorry to bother you. I've been trying to guess what you do for a living. My money's on police inspector.'

The man's expression shifted from startled to amused, and his blue eyes narrowed. 'Near enough. Detective Chief Inspector.'

'Thanks for indulging me. Have a good evening.' She turned to leave, feeling smug at this small victory. It was a skill she liked practising in case she might lose it. This hypervigilance had served her well as a lawyer. Noticing the smallest details could give you an edge over the competition.

'Before you go, tell me how you worked it out.'

'You're not dressed for an office job, and you haven't got the nonchalance of an arty type. You look tetchy and you're trying not to look at your knackered phone – so you're on duty. Doctors are reckless with their health, but they don't tend to smoke. That gives fairly good odds on law enforcement.'

The eyes smiled, and Lucia walked out. The balmy smell of the concrete, the last relic of the sweltering heat just gone, deflected her senses. The street was bathed in a low pink light, and between the buses crawling like fattened red slugs up and down the hill the traffic was thinning out. She felt everything belonged to her alone, and it felt like home.

Chapter 3

The week starting Monday, 31st August (four days before the murder)

The weekend had gone by as if time were running out, and Lucia had barely slept. On the Monday she stood again outside Beatrice Hall, torn between anticipation and an odd hesitance which she tried to suppress. Mrs Byrne let her in, and the heavy doors shut behind them.

Adam was nowhere to be seen. The place was soaked in a pale, early morning light which did it no favours – it only brought up tiny dust particles and intensified its airlessness.

'Come into the kitchen, Lucia, and have a cup of tea before you start. The Professor wants to meet you, and nobody can go through that on an empty stomach.'

Lucia followed Mrs Byrne down the stairs into the basement. The kitchen hadn't changed much during the lifetime of the house. It could have had a certain pared-down, voguish charm, had it not been so downright grotty. At some point in their life the tiled walls must have been white. The butler sinks had grown to an immutable brown, and the red terracotta floor had clearly enjoyed a long existence undisturbed by cleaning devices. Mrs Byrne made two mugs of watery tea and stood there in silence.

'Have you been with the Professor a long time, Mrs Byrne?'

'Longer than I care to remember. Must be going on twenty years now.'

When she estimated the housekeeper had finished her vetting, Lucia said, 'The house is magnificent. Apart from needing some fresh paint, I love how it still has its original features. So many of the buildings around here have been gutted out, which is a shame.'

Mrs Byrne looked newly invigorated, like a tranquiliser had just worn off. 'Oh, you should have seen this place before I arrived. Like a graveyard, it was. I don't know how the Professor could live like that. Mind you, if it weren't for me breaking my back keeping it all in shape, she wouldn't survive a day. Not that she ever leaves that library. With her head in all those dusty books, she wouldn't bat an eyelid if the walls fell down around her.'

That was better. For a moment Lucia thought she'd lost her touch. Her eyes had a grave kindliness that compelled people to open up – it was both useful and exhausting.

'Look at the time. She told me to bring you up to the library at nine.'

Lucia followed the housekeeper. Unusually, the library was on the first floor. Despite its apparent size, the ground floor housed remarkably little living space. The drawing room and the music room were next to each other on the left as you came in through the main door. Straight ahead, across the entrance hall, was the monumental staircase, forking into two at the first landing, and on the right was the rabbit hole descent into the gruesome kitchen.

Mrs Byrne came to a halt outside a pair of panelled doors, which opened into a room overflowing with every type of Victorian feature imaginable – weighty sculptures supporting the bookshelves, stifling purple curtains dragging on the floor and, in the middle, an oppressively carved desk piled high with the equivalent of a university library. 'Professor, Lucia, the decorator, is here to see you.'

'Thank you, Mrs Byrne. I'll call you later if I need you.' From behind the towers of books came a disembodied voice that was low and imposing, with distinctly Slavic tonality. The Professor waited until the door shut to emerge into the light. 'Please, sit.' She gestured to a low armchair next to a side table swamped by reams of handwritten notes. The Professor was in her seventies and moved with practised ease, like a ballerina. A single ornament interrupted the refined plainness of her grey dress – a brooch in the shape of a butterfly, its ample black wings dashed with white. She fixed Lucia with a pair of steely, almond-shaped eyes.

'You're not what I expected.'

'What did you expect?'

'An Essex fishwife.'

'You're not what I expected either. I thought you'd be a batty old woman with bird's nest hair declaiming Shakespeare.'

The Professor burst out laughing, genuinely amused. 'That's a description I have never heard before. Have you always been a decorator?'

'I used to be a lawyer, in a former life. But I don't remember having as many books as you do.'

'Ah yes. My former life.' The tone ruled this out as a subject open to discussion. 'Now, Adam has put the idea into my head that I should have the house renovated. I was doubtful at first, though I must confess I rather like having proper heating, for a change.' The Professor bared her teeth in a condescending smile. 'That boy's not daft. I've no desire to get involved with choosing colours and that sort of thing. Adam tells me you come highly recommended, so impress me. Just don't make lots of noise.'

Lucia had done her research and was relieved at the prospect of being left to her own devices. 'Decorating is a pretty quiet activity. I've drawn up some plans, which I'll leave with you. If you're happy to let me get on with it, then so am I.'

'Good. I'm glad we understand each other. Now, if you'll excuse me, I must get back to my work.' The audience was over.

As Lucia passed the basement stairs, she heard voices from the kitchen. They were faint but unmistakably raised – an argument, but she could only make out broken sentences. As she unloaded her tools from the van, she turned around to glimpse Mrs Byrne standing at the window, wringing her hands. Spotted, the housekeeper scurried away.

The rest of the day as well as the day after were, by comparison, unremarkable. Lucia came and went, working methodically through hardened paint and dried wallpaper. She enjoyed doing this part herself, peeling off each layer to expose another decade of decorative fashion. She liked the 1930s the best. The fine, sharply drawn geometric patterns spoke to her own taste. How ironic, she thought, just when designers had finally shaken off the nauseating burden of the Arts and Crafts, that war should promptly drag them back to floral sentimentality. She saw no one except Mrs Byrne, who dutifully delivered cups of tea on the hour until Lucia begged her to stop. Her face was implacable, bearing no marks of the row. The Professor must have taken meals, though Lucia could not tell when or where. The house was quiet, just as the Professor had asked.

On the third day, as Lucia was scraping away at a particularly revolting wall by the entrance, the doors opened without warning and a woman around Lucia's age, mid-thirties, strode in with a sure step. Her naturally blonde hair was tied back, revealing a face that looked as if it had been drawn with sharp pencil strokes and then gently rubbed out. She was dressed, unexpectedly, in a tweed skirt suit. On anyone older or less attractive it would have looked like period costume, but it suited her fine features and serious demeanour. She met Lucia's eyes with a confident gaze; she was clearly at ease with the place.

'Hello, I'm Lucia.'

'Emilia Poole. Pleased to meet you. I'm Professor Kiseleva's assistant. I'm going to have to be very rude and let you get on. The Professor insists on punctuality.'

Emilia disappeared up the creaky stairs, and Lucia heard the library doors open and close. She was no stranger to being looked down upon in her clients' houses, but she was certain that rudeness wasn't at play here.

'Are you sure you don't want a cuppa? You've been at that wall for hours.' Whatever had upset Mrs Byrne had passed, or at least she had decided to bottle it up.

'Go on then, Mrs Byrne, this time I'm parched. I'll have a break down in the kitchen if I'm not in your way.' Lucia figured that a touch of friendliness laced with information-gathering wouldn't go amiss. She was itching for some juicy gossip that she could share in the Red Lion and to get up Danny's nose. 'I saw Emilia come in just now. She seems nice.'

'Oh yes, Emilia. She's a darling. So well turned out, and always with a friendly smile. Some people treat you like a servant, you know, like you're below them, but not her.'

Lucia felt the compliments didn't quite paint the whole picture but was loath to interrupt the housekeeper in full flow.

'The girl's a saint, putting up with that woman upstairs. She must be bored out of her mind, a pretty young thing like her, spending her days in that musty hole.'

'What exactly does she do, Mrs Byrne?'

'Assistant, the Professor calls her. They sit there for hours, the Professor rambling on and on, and Emilia asks questions and writes things down. The Professor's book, that is. Boring, if you ask me.'

This was a step forward. 'What did the Professor do? Before she retired, I mean.'

Mrs Byrne shot out a bitter look. She didn't seem to hold the Professor's occupation in particularly high regard. 'She was an academic type. One of the London universities – I forget which – they all sound the same to me. Maths. Stuff that makes no sense and is of no use to anyone.'

The housekeeper paused for breath. There was a passing flash of expectancy in her eyes, but her expression almost instantly glazed over. Something was being left unsaid. Lucia waited.

'She barely looked at that poor doting husband of hers. He adored her – she didn't know how lucky she was, and she didn't deserve it. Planning to leave him, she was, before he saved her the trouble and popped his clogs.'

With this last outburst, the relief was complete. Lucia was certain she wouldn't squeeze anything else out of the housekeeper, for now at least. She smiled sympathetically, a reassurance that the confidence was safe with her. 'Thanks for the tea, Mrs Byrne. Best get back to work. That wall isn't going to scrape itself.'

Lucia worked until her fingers were raw and the dull pain in her back became unbearable. Later, stretched out flat on her living room floor, she gave in to all the garbled thoughts. She dragged herself up and looked out of the window. Hampstead High Street was busy with the usual infestation of commuters swarming out of the tube station. The morning's hope had been embodied by the freshly washed hair and scrupulously applied make-up, a spring in their step as they walked into the packed metal lifts. By the end of the day, they were covered in fine black dust and crawled home angry and numb, only to wake up and do it all over again. The rumination gave her perverse pleasure as she remembered this was the life she'd left behind.

Chapter 4

Friday, 4th September (the day of the murder)

The paramedics had bundled up their precious cargo in the hope the Professor might yet be saved. Sensing she was being watched, Lucia turned around. The blue eyes, complete with crumpled chinos, had been on her for some time. It took her a few seconds to place him – the man from the restaurant, the good-looking police inspector.

'The observant decorator. You're everywhere these days.'

'I'd rather not be here, that's for sure.' Lucia sat down on one of the garden chairs, all of a sudden light-headed.

'You're in shock. Where's the kitchen? I'll make you some sugary tea. Guaranteed treatment.'

'I'll be fine. There are others in worse shape.'

'Don't worry about them. The kindly constables are on the case. Besides, nobody ever thinks of the tradesman. Or woman, in this case.'

Lucia laughed feebly. That much was true. After what felt like an eternity he came back with a mug of tea. He must have emptied the whole bag of sugar into it.

'Sorry it took so long. That kitchen's a right mess. I'm Detective Chief Inspector David Carliss, Metropolitan Police.' A badge was flashed. 'And you are?'

'Lucia Steer. I'm the decorator, but you already know that.' She wondered what items of interest had kept him busy in the kitchen.

'I figured as much. Your van's parked outside and you're wearing overalls. Can you tell me what happened?'

Lucia neatly packaged the afternoon into a measured, thorough account, the way she'd been trained to do in her previous life. She wondered whether to go further and decided she had nothing to lose.

'I think the Professor might have been poisoned.'

DCI Carliss, who had been taking copious notes without interrupting, looked up sharply. 'Why do you say that?'

'She was fine. Healthy people don't just collapse. If there had been anything wrong with her, I'd have got a full medical history from Mrs Byrne, blabbermouth as she is. Besides, that glass the Professor was drinking from–'

'Yes, I've seen the glass, thank you,' interrupted Carliss, clearly irked by the unsolicited deductions. 'I think we'd better leave the diagnosis to the professionals, don't you think?'

He put his pen down and patted her on the arm.

'I think you've done more than enough for today. Go home. Have a drink. Have two drinks. I'm certainly going to. Chances are, it could all be very dull. She wasn't young.'

Lucia got up slowly. She didn't like the patronizing dismissal, but she could see he was also trying to put her mind at ease. She felt burned out. For all her bravado, the tragic event had got the better of her.

'On second thoughts, you're in no fit state to be driving. I'll take you back in your van.' The detective marched purposefully ahead, just as she was about to protest. He had a point; she didn't want to do any more thinking today. She handed him the keys and told him the address. He drove prudently, both hands on the wheel, while she weaved in and out of consciousness.

'Will you manage from here?' Carliss said when they had arrived outside her building.

'I'll be fine. Thank you.'

'Well, I'll leave you in peace then. My car's still outside the posh house. Is there a pub nearby that you'd recommend?'

'The Red Lion. Good beer if you don't mind drinking with the local builders.'

'There are worse people I could be drinking with. Thanks. I'll have one for the road.'

The day needed to end. Lucia climbed the stairs to the front door, let herself in and collapsed on the bed rehearsing all that had happened. She got out a bottle of wine and ordered a takeaway. Once her stomach was full and the alcohol had hit, she slept like the dead.

Chapter 5

Friday, 11th September (one week after the murder)

It had been a trying week, and Lucia was glad it was over. Professor Kiseleva had died in the ambulance on the way to hospital. Mrs Byrne said it was heart failure, but no other information had been forthcoming. Lucia stayed away from Beatrice Hall for a few days while the police were combing the place. On her return, the house was even more silent than usual. Everything was preserved exactly as it had been after the ill-fated party. She had half-expected police tape and other such contraptions, but the place bore no trace of the forensic investigation. The housekeeper had confined herself to the kitchen, and Adam was barely ever around. On the rare occasions that he did make an appearance, he was mostly glued to his phone and would vaguely acknowledge Lucia with vacant, glassy eyes when she greeted him. She could only assume he wanted her to continue with the work and so she kept coming back, carrying on as if they hadn't been interrupted by a harrowing death.

That evening, settled on a comfortable bar stool at the Red Lion with a large glass of ice-cold wine, Lucia made a solemn promise to herself that she wouldn't give the Professor's death another thought. If it was a tragic accident, then there was nothing more to be said or done. And if it was something more sinister, then it was none of Lucia's business. It was a police matter, that much had been made clear to her by that uppity inspector.

Sat as she was in the corner furthest away from the door, she was able to watch those coming in without necessarily being noticed. The usual crowd was in attendance, and they were particularly rowdy tonight. Some sort of football-related chat, as far as she could work out. Lucia could have easily gone to one of the other pubs in the area, but the truth was, she liked the atmosphere here – the unfussiness suited her. She certainly wasn't in the mood for an evening alone in her flat.

Her thoughts were interrupted by the latest arrival, who took her entirely by surprise. Detective Chief Inspector Carliss walked in and sat at the other end of the bar from her. He looked like he too had had a very long week. He ran his fingers through his hair and sighed as he eyed up the beers on offer. Becky wasn't working tonight, and Jez, the lad who was taking her place, couldn't pull a pint to save his life, poor thing, and not for want of trying. Lucia watched DCI Carliss order himself some best bitter which Jez managed to spill all over the counter before refilling it twice. The policeman was doing his best to hide the pained look on his face, but that flustered the boy even more. At last, a relatively full glass was placed in front of the customer and money exchanged hands. DCI Carliss breathed a sigh of relief as he took the first, long-awaited sip.

Despite the earlier resolve to keep her nose out of trouble, Lucia just couldn't help herself. She stared in the policeman's direction long enough for him to glance over. As he caught her eye, he looked as if he wanted to make a run for it. Talking to witnesses to a death down the boozer wasn't exactly proper procedure, Lucia mused, not that she planned to let that stop her.

'Hello, Detective Chief Inspector.' She picked up her wine glass, which was nearly empty by now, and walked decisively in his direction. 'Mind if I join you?'

The policeman raised an eyebrow, but he didn't have much of a choice, seeing that Lucia was practically hovering over him, so he gestured to the free stool. 'Miss Steer. Sure, go ahead.'

She perched on the chair with an expectant look on her face. The wine on an empty stomach had spurred her on, and she hadn't had time to think through what she was going to say. DCI Carliss watched her as he sipped his pint. Those piercing blue eyes could be very disconcerting, the way they scanned her face and didn't look away. Lucia shook off an indelicate thought. 'So you took my advice then?'

'What advice would that be?'

'You tried the Red Lion after you dropped me off at home the other day. After we left Beatrice Hall.'

'I did. It's a nice little boozer, this. Not snooty like the rest of the places around here.' The policeman's face stretched into a quizzical smile. 'Feeling better now?'

'Yes, I'm fine, thanks. Sorry for being such a weakling the other day. I don't see many dead bodies in my line of work.'

He laughed. 'No need to apologise. If it makes you feel better, it never gets any easier.'

Lucia brushed back a strand of hair and looked at the empty glasses in front of them. 'Would you like another, Inspector?'

He hesitated for a moment. 'Yes, why not? I'm not on duty tonight.'

Miraculously, Jez succeeded in producing two unscathed drinks. Lucia and DCI Carliss sat for a few moments in what was starting to be a rather companionable silence.

'Have you interviewed everyone then?'

'What do you mean?'

'Everyone who was at the party when Professor Kiseleva died. Have you taken statements from them?'

He patently knew what she meant and was trying to avoid talking about it.

'Yes, obviously. But, as I said, I'm not on duty. I just want a quiet drink before I head home. And I'm not about to discuss confidential police business with you, if that's what you're getting at.'

Lucia turned over in her mind a fresh angle of attack. 'Did you get the tin of poison from the kitchen?'

Carliss sat up very straight, as if she'd just slapped him hard across the face. 'What the… How do you know about that?'

'I've been in the house long enough to know where most things are kept – downstairs at least. Don't look so appalled. It's not like I'm stealing from them. But I can't not notice what's in front of me.'

'So you rummaged around in the kitchen, did you? Fancy yourself as a bit of sleuth?'

She really had managed to step on his toes, she could see that quite plainly. 'Well, you got there first, I'll give you that.' Lucia crossed her arms defiantly as she ploughed on. 'Oh, come on, I'm not stupid. You took your time making that cup of sugary tea for me, didn't you? Had a good snoop around?'

Despite his best efforts to keep up the stern face, the policeman was mollifying. Lucia smiled endearingly – the equivalent of a hand stretched out to the loser in a match. She wasn't trying to be patronizing, but she sensed mutual agreement that she had scored a very good point.

'Sodium fluoroacetate – 1080, as it's commonly known,' she continued. 'Very nasty rat poison. Odourless, tasteless, soluble, no antidote. The symptoms appear to fit. With a large enough dose, you don't stand much of a chance of pulling through. It tends to start with nausea and convulsions, around half an hour after ingestion. After that, you've got an unenviable choice of ends – heart or other organ failure, coma, or septicaemia. If you're lucky, you'll survive with severe brain damage. But I guess you know all this stuff already.'

Carliss sighed in apparent defeat. 'Yes, I do. But before you jump to rash conclusions, it doesn't mean a thing. So they kept rat poison in the kitchen – so what? Doesn't mean the Professor died because she took it.' He stopped himself before he could go any further and breathed in with fresh determination. 'Look, this isn't really on. I can't talk about it in public. It's a police matter. You need to get that in your head once and for all and drop this stupid little Miss Marple act. It's not a game for a bored housewife.'

That kind of brush-off would have made most people lose their rag, but not Lucia. She was determined she wouldn't take the bait. 'For your information, I'm not a bored housewife. I'm not even married. Tell me something else, Inspector. When you spoke to the witnesses, did Mrs Byrne mention the row she had with Adam a few days before the party?'

From the policeman's stony silence, Lucia inferred this was news to him. 'No, I didn't think so. I wonder what else they're hiding, don't you?' she added.

She really did feel sorry for him now. He looked torn – on the one hand dying to find out what else she knew, and at the same time unwilling to get himself entangled into a highly suspect way of uncovering information. In the end, caution won. He downed the rest of his pint and stood up abruptly. 'I think we're done here, Miss Steer. Have a good evening.' And with that, he turned on his heels and walked out without looking back.

Lucia scowled and took another sip of her wine. It hadn't gone as well as she'd hoped. Nonetheless, she had a feeling that this wasn't the last she'd hear of the matter. If all the police could come up with after a whole week was heart failure, there wasn't much of a chance that the inspector could hack it on his own.

Chapter 6

Saturday, 19th September (two weeks after the murder)

It was gone three in the afternoon. Just as the kettle had finished boiling, the shrill sound of the phone ringing on the kitchen table made Lucia jump. She didn't recognize the number but picked it up anyway, involuntarily tense.

'Detective Chief Inspector Carliss here. How're you doing?' The low, purring voice set her mind at rest. She'd half expected to be told that Mrs Byrne or Adam had keeled over. They both managed to look so despondent all the time.

'I'm fine, thanks. I was about to ask how you got my number, but I suppose it is your job.'

'I've got contact details for everyone who was at the Hall.' The line went silent. The inspector's initial confidence had waned, and his hesitation was palpable – he was obviously having second thoughts about whether this was a good idea. At last, he spoke. 'Look, er… OK, this might sound a bit odd. It's not an official call, you understand. I'm not speaking to you right now.'

'But you are, aren't you?' She had to laugh at the absurdity of the situation. He was nervous, that much was clear.

'Yes, of course I am, physically. What I mean is, I'm not speaking to you in my official capacity as a policeman. Can we meet?'

'Sure, do you want me to come down to the station?' teased Lucia, knowing that wasn't what he could possibly have in mind. At the same time, she overrode the imaginary brakes that should have held her back, warning her to stay out of trouble.

The little poke was totally lost on DCI Carliss. 'No, absolutely not. Nowhere public.'

He gave her an address in Kentish Town. She marvelled at its quaintness – two-storey, Georgian, with a bright red door opening straight onto the pavement. It had to be where he lived. She decided to walk all the way, first down to South End Green, where the cacophony of buses and assorted hospital traffic stood in sharp contrast with the haughty emptiness of the windy village streets above. The fashionable resurrected railway cottages of Gospel Oak gradually gave way to tidy, secluded council estates. The latter's fastidious separation of hard surfaces and trimmed greenery brought back memories of hiding places and carefree ballgames. She glimpsed herself as a little girl on a swing, before the days of rubber-floored playgrounds, when knees and elbows would be perpetually covered in half-healed scabs. Those were altogether more innocent times. The estate playgrounds were mostly empty these days.

The policeman's house was one of a cluster overlooking a narrow, cobbled street, like a cardboard cut-out incongruously positioned by a nostalgic town planner. It only had one doorbell.

DCI Carliss opened the door, wearing his predictably unkempt attire. The blue eyes rested on her face –

somewhat timidly, which wasn't how he'd looked at her before.

'You found me OK? Come in.'

The inside was homely but far from prosaic. Carefully selected mid-century items, smooth and clean-lined, were complemented by handsome, lived-in soft furnishings and original watercolours. With the mellow afternoon light streaming in through the tall sash windows, as if through a filter, it was a faultless illustration of domestic contentment. It was evidently his sanctuary. Lucia sank down into a capacious armchair and felt like a child in possession of a coveted invitation to a wealthy neighbour's house.

'I'll make us some tea. Or coffee if you'd prefer?'

'Tea is good. You have a beautiful home. I must admit it's taken me by surprise.' She purposefully affected an easy manner, hoping to put him at ease.

It seemed to work, and he grinned. 'Did you think I lived in a hovel with empty whisky bottles in the kitchen?'

'I did, and I was wrong. This is a proper house.'

'It used to be my parents' house.' He cast a look around, observing it with fresh eyes, and smiled proprietorially. 'I wouldn't be anywhere else.'

Tea came. They sat for a few moments until the atmosphere became awkward. This wasn't a purely social call. 'Do you always invite witnesses to a death round for a cuppa?' asked Lucia.

The inspector shuffled in his seat, a little put out. 'A bit unorthodox, I know. If my boss got wind of this, I'd be out on my ear.' He broke eye contact and stared down at his feet for a moment, gathering his thoughts. 'I thought about what you said the other day in the pub – about the poison under the kitchen sink. To be honest, I haven't thought of much else since. The post-mortem confirmed the Professor had enough 1080 in her to definitively write her off.'

'You're ruling out suicide?'

'I'm not ruling out anything. I'm just setting out the facts. We're treating it as an unexplained death.'

'What does that mean?'

'It means all options are on the table.'

'Is murder one of them?'

'Perhaps. Yes. Along with suicide and accidental ingestion of the poison.'

Lucia blinked. The image of the Professor writhing on the ground refused to leave her brain. 'The Professor wasn't suicidal. And even if she did want to end her life, why choose such a horrendous way to die?'

DCI Carliss didn't reply, but Lucia could tell he didn't have a counterargument. 'It could have been an accident,' he finally offered, though he didn't sound particularly convinced.

'Come off it. How does the rat poison accidentally get out from under the kitchen sink and into the Professor's system?'

'As I said, we can only look at what's in front of us.' Carliss leaned forward in an attempt to regain some ground. 'Listen, if you're to get involved at all – and I'm not saying I'm letting you do that – no one can find out about it.'

'I won't breathe a word.' Lucia had always been partial to a bit of gossip, but this time she knew it was serious. She would keep this to herself – it was a chance she didn't want to blow. She had so desperately hoped that the inspector would come round to the idea that she could be of use. 'What do you want me to do?'

'Just go about your normal business at the Hall. Keep your eyes and ears open.'

'You mean, spy on them?'

'I never said that.'

'But that's what you mean. You're not making much progress with the investigation then?'

The inspector didn't reply.

'I'll take that as a yes, you're not getting anywhere.'

'It's not exactly a priority for the Super,' he said tersely.

'But you think something's off.'

DCI Carliss squirmed a little in his seat and crossed his arms defensively. 'OK, yes. I just don't think it looks right. But that's not enough to justify roping in extra manpower for what could be a wild goose chase.'

'Which is where I come in.'

'Which is where you come in. You look like you could be of use. Nobody ever pays attention to tradespeople, remember?'

The challenge had been laid down, and Lucia could hardly refuse. 'So, what am I supposed to be looking out for?'

'How they're behaving, how they're talking to each other. Anything out of place.'

'You mean, like the argument between Adam and Mrs Byrne?' Lucia couldn't resist bringing that up again.

DCI Carliss pursed his lips. 'Yes, like the *alleged* argument between those two, which may or may not be relevant.'

Lucia leaned into the comfortable armchair and stretched out an arm over the back. 'I'm in. Good call, by the way.'

'What do you mean?'

'Getting me on board. You wouldn't want a civilian solving the murder before you, would you? That wouldn't make you look too good.'

'Unbelievable. Not exactly modest, are you?'

'Modesty gets you nowhere, in my experience. Sharp eyes, however, do.'

'Don't get ahead of yourself. Let's see what you can get for me first,' warned the inspector, drawing his features into the most serious look he could muster under the circumstances.

'So, what's your take on the whole thing? You must have some suspicions, otherwise you wouldn't have got me all the way here.'

'Let's assume for a moment, hypothetically of course–'

'Hypothetically, of course,' Lucia interrupted with a sarcastic smile.

'Let's assume the old bird didn't commit suicide or take the poison accidentally. If she was poisoned with the stuff under the sink, that would make everyone a possible suspect. All of them had access to the tin. And anyone could have slipped the poison into her special fancy glass – no danger of a mix up there. It would either be very stupid, or it would be the perfect murder.'

'In this scenario, whoever killed her would be far from stupid.' Lucia sipped her tea thoughtfully. 'It would be risky though. The execution would have to be faultless.'

She glanced at the policeman. She knew he'd crossed a line, but he looked relieved at the prospect of being able to pour out his thoughts to a sympathetic listener.

It turned out she was right. Carliss pulled out his notebook. 'Let's start with the Professor herself. Alla Kiseleva. She's seventy-eight. In the UK since 1983. Her passport says she was born in Yaroslavl – textbook place, onion domes and all that. She hasn't got dual citizenship, as far as I can tell from the records – we've only got her British passport on file. Shortly after she arrived in this country, she married one Louis Stone, an insurance broker, who died ten years ago. No children. He left her the house and a nice bit of money. Before retiring she worked for the Collaborative Mathematical Society.'

'That rings a bell. It's in Bloomsbury. Left-leaning. Didn't they pride themselves on hiring dissident Russians who managed to get out?'

'That's the one. A bit of a hub for Soviet mathematicians – smart enough to get their hands on the talent when it came their way. Anyway, she started off as a junior researcher and rose up the ranks to Head of Cybernetic Research. Plenty of papers, lecturing, the standard trajectory. I've got my team looking into her background in Russia, so we'll know more shortly. What do you make of her?'

'Before the party, I had only met her once. It was her nephew Adam who hired me. She wasn't rude as such, but she liked to keep her distance. On the face of things, she was obsessed with her work. She was apparently writing a new book on cybernetics. She struck me as imperious and self-centred. I can't imagine she was easy to work for. And there's the business of redecorating the house, of course. It seems money's no object when you're the widow of a rich broker. The Professor left Adam in charge, and he practically hired me on the spot.'

'Interesting. Brings me neatly to a question that's been bothering me all this while. How did you get this job?'

'All the builders around here have had their eye on Beatrice Hall for years. When word came out that it was due for renovation, I tracked Adam down and asked him upfront. It's odd, actually. He gave me the job straightaway. I guess he didn't want to spend too long interviewing tradesmen, just wanted the work to start.'

'You might be right. What's your take on Adam Corcoran?'

'Troubled. Drinker. He lives at Beatrice Hall, as does the housekeeper. As I said before, I heard them having a row a few days before the party. They were down in the kitchen, and I was on the ground floor, so I couldn't make out what they were saying. I'm positive I recognised their voices though. On the day the Professor died, he was talking about selling the Hall. It was the first I heard of it – I suppose that's why he was so set on doing it up. The Professor wasn't best pleased. I also got the impression she wasn't sharing her wealth, although he would have liked her to.'

'People are drawn to money, like flies to the proverbial. How about Mrs Byrne?'

'Quietly angry about something, though I haven't been able to figure out what. She follows Adam around like a fawning puppy. It's pathetic to watch how he strings her along. She doesn't like his drinking habits; it might be she thinks she can save him. She told me she's been with the Professor for twenty years. Nonetheless, there's no love lost between them. Mrs Byrne is always grumbling about the state of the house and boasting how indispensable she is – was – to the Professor.'

Carliss nodded pensively. He was scribbling furiously in his notebook, which was rapidly filling up. Lucia was captivated by the diagrams he had drawn to show the connections between the characters, like a mind map of mistrust.

'What's the story with the young woman?' he continued.

'Emilia. She's the Professor's assistant. It sounds like she's been tasked with the donkey work on the book – research, typing, proofreading. She was on good form at the party. With me, she's polite but reserved – but then, I'm not a man, nor susceptible to schoolgirl charm. She strikes me as a touch old for such an entry-level job. Not to mention being at the Professor's beck and call.'

'The doctor?'

'Outwardly pleasant, for which read reptilian. Probably ex-military.'

'What were the couple called?'

'The Walkers. John and Margaret. Run-of-the-mill Hampstead types. Barrister and stay-at-home wife. Unremarkable at first sight, but these people always are. They'll have a handsome period house done in graceful shades of white, the kind that photographs well. Nevertheless, as soon as they're finished with it, they'll want to change it all again – the wife, that is. Displacement activity for the lack of purpose that's gnawing away at her.'

'Ouch. That's harsh. I'm sure you've seen plenty like them in your line of work.' He put the notebook to one side and stretched out his legs. 'To be honest, this whole business is one big headache.'

He didn't look like someone with a headache – he looked thrilled to bits. You're as bad as I am, Lucia judged. Just can't resist a challenge.

The inspector finished his tea and fixed her with newly found determination. 'How about an actual drink? I think we've earned it.'

Lucia laughed, and found herself unusually relaxed. 'OK, but only if you promise not to talk about this wretched death.'

'Deal. I know a pub just round the corner with dubious carpet and excellent wine. Will that do?'

'Perfect,' she replied instantly – after all, it wasn't every day that she met a policeman as eccentric as this one was.

Chapter 7

They walked out onto the anachronistic cobbles, and the day revealed itself in all its glory, like a saccharine pathetic fallacy. The pub was a mere hundred yards away, but they ambled slowly, delectably, savouring every step. In eighteenth-century Kentish Town, nothing could go wrong on a hazy, warm Saturday afternoon. They settled at a table outside, gulping first mouthfuls like holy water.

'What did you do before you became a decorator?'

'How do you know I haven't always been a decorator?' retorted Lucia with a playful smile.

'Oh, give me a break. You don't exactly sound like those geezers down the Red Lion.'

Lucia turned her face to the sun. 'I used to be a lawyer.'

'City type, I assume?'

'Why do you say that?'

'Too arrogant to be anything else.'

'I'll take that as a compliment.'

'Suit yourself. Why did you jack it all in?'

She found she didn't mind the interrogation. 'It's a thankless line of work. You're only in it for the money, but you never get to spend it because you're so busy slaving away for all sorts of shady types. I've always been good with my hands, so decorating felt like a good get-out.'

DCI Carliss tilted his head, somewhat puzzled. 'You are something else. When you said you're good with your hands, I would have thought baking or sewing, you know, the popular stuff that disillusioned posh girls get into. Isn't it weird to be the only woman with all these macho blokes around you?'

'I don't mind it. They're easy enough to handle. Besides, I can barely boil an egg, and I've never sewn anything in my life. I thought I might become a mechanic, but you need to do a qualification, and frankly I'm sick of those. I can fix a car anyway, so I thought I could be a decorator and, if the van breaks down, most of the time I know what to do. And you? A copper with an inherited pile in North London and no regard for procedure? Where does that fit in?'

It was the detective's turn to affect an air of mystery. As his expression turned to an easy smile, Lucia twigged that he was gently poking fun at her. 'I figured I've got nothing to lose. If I get sacked, I'll have had a good run of it. The only thing I care about is getting to the bottom of the case. And as to the house, my parents worked for the Home Office. Jobs for life, as it used to be in those days. Mind you, when they bought the house in the late 1960s, this area was rough. But they were blissfully happy, a young couple starting out, with their own place to call home. When they died, I couldn't bear the thought of the house being sold, so I moved back in.'

'Isn't it unsettling, living as an adult in your childhood home?' Lucia recalled how swiftly she had forsaken her own nest. People moved on – that's what adulthood was all about.

'I made it my own. Before, I was flitting from one rented flat to another, tracing my way across the city, like everyone does when they start out. In the end, my old village drew me back. And you? Oh, indulge me briefly.

Rented flat in Hampstead. Nobody in that block stays for longer than a year or speaks to any of their neighbours. Rich parents in Hampshire. You head back occasionally, but they're disappointed you gave up a stellar legal career for manual labour, so you avoid them like the plague. Pony, boarding school, the lot. Just not enough affection.'

Lucia couldn't suppress an inner smile that she hoped hadn't travelled to her lips. He'd missed the mark by a long shot. 'Yes, something like that. Don't feel too sorry for me, will you?'

The blue eyes narrowed. He had probably worked out she was pulling his leg as he changed tack. 'Another one?'

Lucia caught a glimpse of her watch. They had seamlessly moved into early evening, as if there had been a moratorium on time. How bizarre to have spent so long, and not notice, with someone she barely knew. She fruitlessly sought to conjure up a reason to leave – an appointment, a date, a class. Her mind was wilfully blank. Ultimately, there was nothing to lose.

'Go on then.'

The second glass of cold wine erased all her misgivings, and she decided to give free rein to her curiosity. 'What made you become a copper?'

Carliss glanced sideways into the light, just like Lucia had done moments earlier, and she sensed he hadn't yet made up his mind on how much of himself to disclose. She knew she baffled him with the strange mix of artless and unreadable that she affected. He seemed like the kind of man who had spent his life sheltering from excessively strong feelings that might threaten to rattle his equilibrium.

He finally answered. 'I felt this strong sense of duty. I know it sounds clichéd. My parents instilled it in me. I'm not a stickler for rules, as you may have gathered already, but I'm a firm believer in basic decency. Plus, I wasn't brainy enough to be a doctor.'

'I find that hard to believe. I think you enjoy the power you wield. Having the psychological advantage.'

'Yes, I admit I do. I don't use it for nefarious purposes, so that's me absolved.'

Lucia couldn't resist carrying on with her assessment of the policeman. 'How come you haven't risen any higher than Detective Chief Inspector, at your age?'

She waited to see if she'd gone too far – if he would take offence at the impertinent line of questioning. She had a habit of directness which most people – especially men – found disconcerting.

To her relief, the corner of his mouth lifted into a relaxed smile, as if he'd been expecting the question all along. 'I like working in the field, not sitting behind a desk writing polite emails and sucking up to the boss. I couldn't care less about getting promoted.'

And so it meandered, pleasurably, on and on, until a decision loomed.

'Hungry?'

In her head, she hesitated for a split second, but the reply shot straight out. 'Famished.'

By now, all prudence had gone to the winds, the way it does, deliciously, when you've got a bottle of wine and not much else swirling around your stomach. Carliss knew a quaint little French restaurant a few streets away, a home from home for hankering Parisians who had got waylaid on the pilgrimage trail to Kensington. They ate, drank and talked until they were unceremoniously turfed out at midnight.

'Good night, Miss Steer.'

'Good night, Detective Chief Inspector.'

'David.'

'Good night, David. And thank you for a very nice evening.'

He teetered on the step but thought better of it.

They parted.

Chapter 8

It was past ten o'clock when Lucia finally stirred. Shards of light streamed into the darkened bedroom along the edges of the blind. She quickly ran over the events of the previous evening in her head and was relieved she'd kept her wits about her. It would have been pretty bad form if she'd ended up in bed with the copper investigating her former client's death – even though he did have very nice eyes and she had genuinely considered it a few times.

With plenty of strong coffee inside her, Lucia's senses sharpened. All roads led to the Professor, and yet she eluded their grasp. To make any sense of her death, they had to start with an element of certainty. Where the Professor had come from was an unknown. Where she had landed, however, was not, so the logical first point of call was the Collaborative Mathematical Society. If the Professor's work had really been all-encompassing, she was likely to have left deep footprints there. More importantly, Lucia relished the prospect of getting one up on the DCI.

A near perfect straight line joined her flat to the destination, Montague Street, where the Society was protectively tucked under a wing of the British Museum.

The 168 was waiting patiently for her at the bottom of Rosslyn Hill and duly deposited its cargo on Southampton Row. Booth's poverty map had categorised the area as predominantly red, with smatterings of yellow on the Squares, Bedford and Russell – middle class, well-to-do, with touches of upper-middle and upper classes, wealthy. Montague Street was definitely in the former category – respectable, though categorically out of the price range of the middle class. Every other door marked the entrance to an overpriced hotel that unsuccessfully tried to distinguish itself from its neighbouring rivals. They all had dingy basement dining rooms with litter piled up outside the windows.

The Society was in the same category, with its yellow stock brick darkened by two centuries of man-made grime and indistinguishable from the rest of the row, except for a matt brass plaque announcing its name to the world. Lucia had done her research – the Society was open to the general public on a Sunday. If they couldn't yet determine what kind of person the Professor was in private, Lucia wanted to at least craft a picture of who the woman was professionally. She also hoped there would be one or two members of staff that she could gently interrogate – if she was particularly lucky, perhaps even someone who had been there long enough to remember the Professor.

The doorbell rang timidly. No answer. The second ring was cut short by the slow-motion opening of the door. In the dimly lit entrance hall stood a man somewhere in his eighties who looked like he might fall apart at the lightest touch. He wore a dated suit that was a few sizes too big for his emaciated body.

'Hello. You're open today, aren't you?' Lucia beamed her most endearing smile.

The man shuffled uneasily from one foot to the other, looked her up and down a few times and computed the level of danger as low.

'Yes, yes, we are. Come in, come in.' His manner shifted to mild embarrassment, perhaps at how unkempt the interior promised to be, but was shortly overcome by an eagerness to please. 'I do apologise. Sundays are visiting days, but I can't remember the last time anyone turned up. I didn't catch your name. Herbert Jennings is mine. I look after this place. Everyone here calls me Herb.'

'Pleased to meet you, Herb. I'm Lucia Steer.'

'Delighted to make your acquaintance, Lucia. This way. I have to sign you in before I let you loose in the library. All this health and safety business. Nonsense, if you ask me. If there's a fire, you just run for it. Putting your name down in the book won't save you.' He doddered ahead, switching on the lights as he went. The entrance hall was more attractive than first impressions had suggested. With an experienced eye, Lucia admired the tasteful stone-coloured walls, not long painted, and the precious chandelier.

The bureaucratic requirements were ticked off in a cramped, windowless room carved out of what could only have been a broom cupboard. Its door dismissively bore the label "Caretaker", leaving no doubt about the purpose of the dingiest space in the building. Once formalities were out of the way, Herb ushered her back into the hall and through a pair of imposing panelled doors. He stood back proudly as he opened them to unveil the pièce de résistance. It stood in clear contrast to the last library Lucia had been in. This one was light and airy, painted in a richly pigmented green. The shelves were sturdy but pared back, of a recent design that paid homage to the original space but didn't copy it. Lucia brushed her hand against one of the armchairs that rested on the softly carpeted floor.

'It's wonderful. I could while away hours in here. What a superb job you've done, taking care of this place so well.'

Herb puffed up like a venerable peacock, nearly filling his suit. 'It's the best library in London, if not the South East. I would say the country, but the Bodleian might object. Oh, you should have seen it before we smartened it up. But the money came in very handy, and just at the right time. So good of her...' He stopped mid-sentence, not exactly upset, but ostensibly stirred.

'Who paid for it?'

He regained his composure. A keen flicker in his eyes indicated he was anxious to unburden himself. She was good at coaxing out people's internal monologues. The honest eyes always did the trick.

'Oh dear, I don't know if I'm supposed to be blathering on to strangers.'

She couldn't lose him, not now. 'With things you want to get off your chest, it's sometimes easier to talk to a kind stranger, who won't judge.'

The respite was almost palpable. Now he had given himself the green light to open up, there was no stopping him.

'The Professor. That's what everybody called her. Professor Alla Kiseleva. She was so generous when it came to the institute.' It was an unnecessarily pompous way to describe the place, no doubt born out of long-standing exposure and the necessity for self-affirmation. 'She was in a class of her own. Not just brains – she had plenty – but an air, an elegance about her. Mind you, she could destroy you with a single stare when she was so minded. I saw her take down more than one unsuspecting sod who dared argue with her. I do miss her, I must say, since she retired.'

Lucia was reluctant to step in. At the same time, the revelation was of considerable importance, and pertinent questions had to be asked.

'Herb, I've got some very upsetting news, I'm afraid. I used to work for the Professor. She died a couple of weeks ago.'

His already ashen face showed genuine heartbreak. It was touching that he cared about a woman who, by all appearances, had failed to forge any emotional attachment to those closest to her.

'I'm alright. Just a funny turn. I can't believe she's gone. I suppose none of us is getting any younger.'

'I'm so sorry. It's a big shock for you. Especially when you knew her so well.' She hesitated slightly before releasing the next, vital detail. She didn't want to miss any element of his reaction. 'It doesn't look like the cause of death was natural.'

She watched Herb crumple into his baggy suit. He suddenly looked like he was going to vanish altogether, like a cheap magic trick. He wobbled over to an armchair and tumbled down, head in his hands. When he eventually reappeared, the pallor of his face could give any death mask a run for its money. When he spoke, his voice was quiet and croaky, as if from beyond the grave.

'You're saying someone killed her? That's impossible. Why would anyone want to do that? How did she die? And how do you know all this?' His expression was gradually turning hostile, and Lucia feared he was yet again slipping through her fingers.

'She hired me to paint her house. I'm a decorator, you see. I was there when she died. It was awful. The police suspect it was poison, but it hasn't been confirmed yet. And I don't know why someone would want her dead. I came here hoping I'd come across something that will help me find out. Nobody deserves to go like that.'

Herb lifted his head a touch, like an ancient tortoise tentatively peeking out of its shell. Lucia hoped her honesty would disperse any suspicions on his part. She had to cling on to him. He was the first source of information on the Professor she had encountered who was unlikely to have an ulterior motive.

'I don't know what to tell you. She was well liked here, on the whole. I remember crystal clear the day I met her. It was 1983, just before we were due to break up for Christmas. She came to be interviewed for a researcher position. I said a little prayer for her as she went in. The then-President terrified the life out of his underlings, but she had him right where she wanted him. She was beautiful, there's no doubt about that, and he was a man, but more than that, she had this natural authority. Bossy and confident. When she smiled, it was like the sun shone on you, and you were the only person in the room. She won him over, and he gave her a job. It turned out the institute was her natural home. She spent more hours here than any of the others – long days, even long nights reading and writing papers. She lectured and published as if she was running out of time. But nobody here would want to hurt her.'

'You said she was liked, on the whole. Was there anyone who didn't share that feeling?'

Herb seemed slighted at the very suggestion. The Professor was evidently skilled at harnessing loyalty when she was so inclined.

'Everyone liked her.' He repeated his statement, though a little less convincingly this time. 'There was this one senior researcher. When she joined the institute, he was the only one who voted against her. You see, we have this rather particular system for letting new members join. Old-fashioned, you could say, like barristers' chambers. The President gets first dibs at interview. If they like the candidate, they recommend them to the existing members, who get to snoop through the CV and intimidate the newcomer over a fancy lunch. At the end of the lunch, once all the booze has been consumed, the members write their vote on a piece of paper and put it in the ballot box. Not many make it through. She held her own and did, bar one vote – Dr Oleg Ivanov's, a fellow countryman, of all people. He said he had read in the original the articles she had submitted as samples of her work. The language was clumsy and stilted, he said, like they'd been written by someone subconsciously translating but not interpreting. He mocked her in front of the President – for all the knowledge she claimed she had, she couldn't write proper Russian. It didn't matter in the long run, but they never saw eye to eye. He never said anything to her face, but gossip travels fast. You don't think it could be him, do you? He retired around the same time that she did. I've heard he lives quietly in Clapham, gardening and waiting to die, like we all are.'

The lengthy speech had obviously worn him out, and Lucia decided to call it a day. 'You've been incredibly helpful, Herb. I know it's hard, but I really appreciate your talking to me. I want to find out who did this to Professor Kiseleva. Do you think I can have a look at her work?'

'Of course. Everything she published is here, in the library. She wasn't appointed Head of Cybernetic Research for nothing. See for yourself – here, on your left.'

The Professor's output was neatly catalogued. Much of it had been bound, including what appeared to be her magnum opus, *Cybernetics in the Soviet Consciousness – A Critical Approach*, a polished version of her doctoral thesis. The rest consisted of journal articles, largely a rehash of her doctorate in pot-boiler instalments, book reviews and lecture notes. They were written in passably academic English of the bland variety that permeated the higher education environment – devoid of irony or idiomatic nuance. So far, so unremarkable. Nonetheless, Dr Ivanov's snipe troubled Lucia. It was a strangely specific gripe to have with a newcomer.

'You don't happen to have Dr Ivanov's address? I'd very much like to talk to him.'

'It'll be in the records. But I'm not allowed to give it out. Data protection, they call it.' He didn't sound particularly convinced.

'Oh, I know. Such a nuisance, this data protection stuff. You know, the other day I phoned the GP surgery for my mum's test results – she's deaf as a post, bless her – and guess what they said. We're not authorised to give out personally sensitive information. What did they think I was going to do with it? Ludicrous, if you ask me.'

Herb smiled, persuaded, as the shared injustice spurred him on. 'Tell me about it. These days, you can't even pick up a parcel without a piece of paper vouching that you're who you say you are. You know what – it'll be our little secret.' He winked and scrambled to his office. After much leafing of a greasy ledger, he shouted out triumphantly, 'Ah yes, here he is. If he's still with us, that is.'

'Thanks, Herb, you've been an absolute star. I owe you a stiff cup of tea next time I see you, or a stiff anything of your choice.'

Herb beamed out of his carapace. 'Lovely to meet you, despite the circumstances. Careful, I might have to hold you to that.'

'It would be my pleasure.'

It was a good plan to leave on a high note. Besides, there was some South London sleuthing to do. Lucia said her lengthy goodbyes – Herb was unwilling to part from company he was unlikely to enjoy again any time soon – and jumped on the underground. She had no plan beyond knocking on Dr Ivanov's door and asking him the obvious questions outright.

The house was one of a snaking row of nineteenth-century carpenters' cottages which had been recently elevated to accommodation for the professional classes. It was instantly recognisable even before Lucia saw the door number, being the only one without a modishly painted front door. The patch of grass at the front was missing the touch of a lawnmower. She rang the doorbell and waited for what seemed like an eternity.

The door was opened by a well-fed woman anywhere between thirty and fifty, complete with pink velour tracksuit, curled blonde hair, and laboriously applied eyelashes.

'Hello. My name's Lucia. I'm looking for Dr Oleg Ivanov.'

'Hello, love. Well, you're a bit late. He passed away a couple of years ago. What business have you got with him?'

'I've come to bring news about a mutual friend. Someone he used to work with.'

'Oh, that. Yes, he was always talking to me about his work. Not that I understood any of it, mind you. It came with the job, caring for him, that is. And I did it well, if I do say so myself. He was an easy one, I must say. No trouble at all – up early, at his desk and writing, then reading in his chair and only wanting plain little meals. No trouble at all. I was chuffed when he left me this place. Didn't see it coming. Though you do think, all this time wiping his you-know-what, I deserve something for it, don't I? He took care of me in the end. No family to leave it to, so it would have been a waste, nice house like this.'

The long stream of verbal diarrhoea was very welcome since it saved further questioning. Lucia was running out of steam – it was early afternoon, and she hadn't had a chance to stop for lunch. Besides, she was itching to share her findings with Carliss. She found herself having imaginary conversations with him, filling him in on her findings, and berated herself for it. She didn't need his approval.

'I'm sorry to hear that he's gone. Well, I'll be off then. Thanks for your help.'

Typical, that it should be a dead end. After the initial elation of pursuing an exciting lead, Lucia was deflated. Still, what she had unearthed about the Professor was serious food for thought.

Chapter 9

There wasn't anything Lucia was particularly keen to do, nowhere she had to go. The prospect of returning to her empty flat and whiling away the hours until she fell asleep didn't really appeal. The Red Lion would be the perfect place to have a quiet drink and regroup. She was wrong. The pub was far from empty. Luckily, the crowd had spilled outside, cigarettes and vapes in hand. The clientele was the same as on a Friday, minus the ones who hadn't been able to escape weekend family duties. The average age was early twenties – old enough to be drinking legally, young enough to live with their parents and be desperate to get out of the house after Sunday lunch.

Becky smiled conspiratorially from behind the bar. Lucia had her down as a good sort. She was nineteen and invariably looked picture-perfect, halfway between Old Hollywood and second-rate adult movie. Newcomers would often mistake her appearance for availability but were soon put right. Becky had a boyfriend in the Marines and a low threshold for suggestive comments.

'Alright, Lucia? You're not going to turn me down this time, are you?'

'No, I'm definitely here to drink. Pour away.'

Becky fetched a large glass of the white Burgundy and stirred herself a sickly concoction of flavoured gin and tonic. It was the weekend for her too, after all.

'Busy for a Sunday, isn't it?'

'Nah, this lot are always in here. Nothing better to do, I suppose. No chores, no kids. Might as well have a good time before they've got to be back at the grindstone tomorrow. Cheers then. I hear you got the big house. Not that it makes a difference, now the old bat's gone.' Becky leaned over, her gravity-defying false eyelashes quivering like giant spiders. 'I hear you were there when she died. What was it like?'

'Pretty awful. She must have been in a lot of pain. They took her to the hospital straight away, not that it made any difference.'

'It's mental. Like something you read about in the papers, but you never think you'd see it on your own doorstep.' Becky looked more titillated than terrified, like she'd magically stepped into a popular crime drama. 'And the coppers turned up. They don't just drop in on every single person who's kicked the bucket. They obviously think something fishy's going on.'

'Yes, I spoke to them. Adam was there too.' Lucia left it there, hoping Becky would stay true to form and fill in the information gap.

'Adam? Ooh, that's exciting. Maybe he's the one who bumped her off. Doesn't strike me as the killing type. But then again, it's always the quiet ones you've got to watch out for. The ones who don't look like they've got it in them.' She was off on a wander in her imaginary murder mystery. 'Getting him in to do all her dirty work and stringing him along like that. He must have just snapped.'

'What do you mean, stringing him along?'

'Oh, you know, everyone's gossiping about it around here. He's like her butler or something, running the house, doing all her errands, except he's not getting paid for it. Or not getting paid enough. He spends plenty of time drinking the bar dry in here, and that's not cheap. Mind you, he must have a day job. Always wearing that suit. He and Danny were having a good old chinwag in the corner the other day. I heard Adam whinging that he's got no money. Tight old cow. It's not like she was poor, with a pile like that.'

So, Adam and Danny hadn't just 'bumped' into each other down the pub. 'Who does Adam talk to when he's in here, Becky?'

'Just Danny, now I think of it. They don't spend too long together normally. Just a swift pint and Danny's off. Adam's the one who hangs around afterwards, drowning his sorrows. Speak of the devil. Pint of IPA, Adam?'

Adam crawled in with his usual funereal look. He briefly acknowledged Lucia, but his eyes were glazed over, like he was in a trance. 'Thanks, Becky. I'm just going to sit down and do some work. Do you mind bringing it over?'

Lucia wondered what sort of work this was. He didn't have a laptop or notebook with him.

'Told you. That man's got guilt written all over his face.' Becky had cast herself as the lady detective, and she clucked with delight. 'Only a matter of time till he goes down. Better bring him his pint. One of his last.' For all her practised façade, her childish delight betrayed the fact that she was still very young.

Distracted by Becky's career aspirations, Lucia failed to notice Adam had been on the phone all this time. The conversation had started out as civilised, but before too long he was hissing angrily, doing his best to keep his voice down to avoid being heard. His sallow face had been upgraded to an aubergine shade of purple and was dotted with sweat. Lucia thought she could make out a meaningless 'What was I supposed to do?' He put the phone down and slurped his nearly full pint before heading to the toilet.

Becky's mouth was half open with a logically faultless interpretation of Adam's predicament when she was interrupted by the slam of the door behind the bar. The landlady was out of her lair, scanning her surroundings with the meticulousness of a sniper. She narrowed in on her target and poured herself a large glass of the Burgundy.

'Lucia, how wonderful to see you. It's been too long. How have you been holding up? Such a nasty business at Beatrice Hall. You must be traumatised.'

Leila was mad as a box of frogs at the best of times. By all accounts, she was wholly within her rights – better a dipsomaniac in Hampstead than under house arrest in the Middle East. She prided herself on only having spent one of her nine lives, namely when she packed up a bag and fled across the Turkish border in the early 1980s. What happened before she left and how she lived since arriving in London were bottomless sources of inconsistent stories. She never spoke of the part in between. The most enduring relic of her origins was her dress sense, an unrepentant tribute to one of the more culturally insensitive *Carry On* films.

'I'm fine. Horrible business, Becky and I were just saying.'

Leila draped herself theatrically on the bar and inhaled most of the glass in one fell swoop. 'They say it was' – she paused for maximum effect, fixing them with dilated pupils under the heavy make-up – 'MURDER!' She took a deep breath and squinted. 'I remember another case like it, up by the ponds. Woman was found hacked to death in her own house. Perhaps a serial killer is on the loose.' Her eyes widened – if any further widening was physically possible. 'We shouldn't be out and about. We could be in mortal danger!'

This was ridiculous even by Leila's standards. The stock of Burgundy must be nearly depleted at this rate, thought Lucia.

'I wouldn't worry, babe. It looks like it was one of her own that did her in.' Becky was back in the game and eager to publicise her deductions. 'I reckon it's Adam.'

Leila nodded frantically in approval, as thrilled as Cleopatra before her milky bath. 'Of course! So clever of you, Becky. He's got that look about him. Shifty and intense. He must be the mass murderer.'

Lucia didn't want to point out that the chances of a serial killer being on the loose were close to nil. The incident of the dead woman that Leila brought up was undoubtedly macabre and had made the rounds in the neighbourhood. However, since there was no way the police could have charged a starving Alsatian, the case – along with the unfortunate animal – had been put to rest.

Before a more plausible version of the Professor's death could be put forward, the women were interrupted by Adam returning from his excursion. 'Can I get another, please?'

'Coming right up,' Becky said. 'I'm with you, Leila. I bet he's not right in the head. A psychopathic mass murderer.'

As Becky and Leila continued exchanging increasingly fantastical theories, Lucia watched him. The pallor was still there, but he seemed revitalised. He focused intently on the screen of his phone, his foot tapping under the table. The shrill ring of her own device startled her. It was Carliss. She decided she would let it go through to voicemail. She didn't want to risk talking to him with an audience, even with Becky and Leila engrossed in their respective monologues. No sooner had the ringing stopped that she listened to his message.

'Hi, Miss Steer. Hope I didn't keep you up too late the other night. Sorry to call you on a Sunday, but I thought you'd want to know. I've just got off the phone to forensics. There was no poison of any kind in the champagne. Not on the Professor's glass, nor anywhere else. Seems like we were on the wrong track all along. Meet me at Beatrice Hall tomorrow morning, first thing. We need to get to the bottom of this.'

Chapter 10

In the morning, on the narrow road outside Beatrice Hall, life was carrying on undisturbed. Couriers, builders, parents, nannies and children scooted past, unsuspecting, unaware. The van screeched to a halt and was expertly manoeuvred into an impossibly tight spot right in front of the house. It narrowly missed an offensively stinky refuse bag perched precariously on the kerb. Despite the eye-watering rents, the blocks of flats housing families with droves of small children didn't tend to come with adequate bin provision. The whole episode managed to impress the Polish builders on the scaffolding next door, so much that they forgot to wolf-whistle when Lucia got out.

Uncharacteristically, the outer gate was unlocked and slightly ajar. The steps up to the entrance were cluttered with the debris of dry leaves and petals that heralded the arrival of autumn. What was left of the flower border bore the dejected look of abandonment. Now that its mistress was gone, the house was unloved – Mrs Byrne had to all appearances given up.

When Lucia got to the top of the stairs, the door opened with perfect timing and she was greeted by DCI Carliss, whose face broadened into a smile. 'Thank goodness you're here. This place gives me the creeps. I hope they're paying you well for it.'

'They will be if I ever get the work done. I've got some news to share.' Lucia was more thankful to see him than she would have liked.

'So do I. That's why I called out of the blue. Let's settle in first.'

They walked through the overbearing doors and stood in the entrance hall. There was no sign of Mrs Byrne – she must have been in a bad way after the death and the consequent upheaval.

Carliss said, as if reading Lucia's mind, 'The nephew and the housekeeper are around, but we should be pretty safe for a while. I'm about to interview them, so they're probably hiding in their respective cubbyholes, getting anxious. Shall we?'

They went through to the cavernous drawing room with its blistering gold pillars. The heavy wallpaper was peeling in places, and the paint had turned a chain-smoking yellow. Lucia opened the French doors for some fresh air, and in doing so inadvertently glanced at the spot where the Professor had collapsed. Against the serene backdrop of the garden, it didn't seem real. Outside, with school drop off and the commuter rush hour nearing their end, the noise of the traffic had subsided, replaced with a dull whirr of a drill. Home renovation was a beloved local sport that could be practised in all weathers since it could be so conveniently outsourced and expertly directed from the comfort of a crisp office or a yoga studio.

Carliss launched himself into a shabby armchair. 'We've got the tin from under the kitchen sink – if we're dealing with a killer, let's hope they've left something of themselves behind. What makes no sense is that there's no 1080 anywhere else – in her glass, on the other glasses, on the crockery, cutlery, food, drink, you name it, they've tested everything. It takes about thirty minutes for the first effects of the poison. She collapsed at five thirty-five.

Even assuming a delayed reaction, she couldn't have ingested it earlier than four thirty. We know she was at the party, in full sight of everyone, since around four. Nobody remembers her going back into the house during that time. So, unless we're missing a trick, we've got ourselves an impossible death.'

Since Lucia had last seen him, he seemed to have acquired two deep furrows cutting across his forehead. He looked like he was taking the case very personally, like a specially crafted puzzle that he was under intense pressure to crack.

'In case you were wondering, the timing of the death rules you out,' the inspector added with a self-satisfied smirk. 'You'd only just got back to the house when she collapsed, so there's no way you could have administered the poison.'

'You weren't seriously suspecting me, were you?' gasped Lucia incredulously.

'No, not really, but I've got to keep my eyes peeled, haven't I? All in a day's work.' He looked through his well-thumbed notebook. 'We can discount suicide. I suppose she could have had the 1080 on her and slipped it into her mouth when nobody was looking. But traces would have been found in her pocket. Or a wrapper with traces of poison would have been found somewhere in the house or the garden. She could conceivably have disposed of the wrapper in some ingenious way that escapes me right now, but that's really pushing it. Any bright ideas?'

Lucia racked her brains, trying to lure out a niggling image that had stuck in her subconscious. The Baccarat coupe that the Professor was drinking from was so distinctive from the others. It was as if someone was taunting them with the obvious solution, only to snatch it away by making it unfeasible. 'Do you think you can get me the Professor's champagne glass from police evidence? Just for us to examine ourselves, and then you can sneak it straight back.'

Carliss was baffled. 'Well, yes, I suppose I could. Nobody else is looking at the case right now, so I should be able to get away with it. But I don't see what it's going to add if forensics have already been all over the glass. I suppose two more pairs of eyes won't hurt. Your turn now. What's the news?'

Lucia savoured the anticipation of recounting the outcome of her trip to Bloomsbury, secretly pleased with herself for taking the initiative to play detective. Her resolve to leave her former life behind was being seriously undermined. She hoped the inspector wouldn't reprimand her for going further than the brief she'd been assigned, but she figured that by now he had little choice.

The policeman's eyes did widen, but by the end he looked more impressed than annoyed. 'Bloody hell. I should be angry, shouldn't I? I told you to listen, not to ferret around. But I've got to hand it to you – you've done some excellent work. Better than most of the sergeants I've trained over the years, all pointless diplomas and not an ounce of common sense between them. You'll have me out of my job at this rate,' he added with a wink. 'She's a very slippery character, our Professor. I've got some contacts left in the Home Office – people I met through my parents, and who've owed me a few favours over the years. I'll see if they can get hold of anything that might enlighten us.'

'There's something else. After the visit to Clapham, I went back to the Red Lion. Adam was there and acting very strangely. Something is going on that is severely unsettling him,' Lucia said. She pondered whether to mention Adam's regular tête-à-têtes with Danny but decided to hang on to that fact for now – she didn't see how it was relevant to the Professor's death. 'According to the barmaid, who doesn't miss much, he's got serious money trouble. It seems the Professor wasn't being especially generous with her factotum.'

‘Hmm. I’ll see what I can shake out of him, and that funny housekeeper of theirs. Right, I’d better go find them both. Are you OK to hang around till I’m done, so I can fill you in on all the dirt?’

‘Of course. I wouldn’t dream of going anywhere.’ Lucia had plans of her own – some quiet snooping upstairs while the interviewees were detained.

Chapter 11

The basement stairs creaked, signalling that the two witnesses were heading out of the kitchen. Carliss went ahead to meet them. Lucia busied herself examining a wall just outside the drawing room where she could get a good view. Adam was the first to emerge, followed by Mrs Byrne's dragging steps. Their faces bore the marks of sleep deprivation – unsurprisingly, given the recent horror they had experienced. Lucia couldn't be absolutely certain from her vantage point, but she thought she could detect another sentiment – guilt, laced with a touch of fear.

Carliss gave the uneasy-looking duo a comforting smile. 'Mrs Byrne, Mr Corcoran. I do apologise to have kept you. Thank you for agreeing to meet with me, and I'm sorry for having to intrude again at such a difficult time. I know you've already given your statements, so I'll do my best to avoid repetition. Mrs Byrne, would you please follow me to the drawing room? Mr Corcoran, I won't keep you long.'

Adam loitered behind them, unsure what to do with himself. Lucia seized the opportunity and narrowed in. 'Hello, Adam. How are you holding up?'

He jumped. 'Lucia, I didn't see you there. You startled me. I'm as well as can be, under the circumstances. It's awful. I just can't stop thinking of poor Auntie suffering like that.' He didn't appear altogether convinced by his own predicament.

'I know this is probably the last thing on your mind, but have you thought what you want to do about decorating? I'd assumed you wanted me to carry on, so I've been turning up as usual, but I totally understand if you want to call it off.'

He looked perversely cheered up by the change of tack and scanned the entrance hall with scarcely concealed satisfaction. 'On the contrary. In fact, I'm glad you've mentioned it. I was going to call you, but since you're here, even better. I'd very much like you to carry on with the work.'

'No problem. I'd be very happy to stay on if you'd like me to and if I'm not intruding.'

'Thanks, Lucia. Don't be daft, you're not intruding. If I'm honest, it's nice to have another soul around the place. The house is far too big for me and Mrs B.'

Lucia made a mental note of the exchange as extremely informative. She didn't delude herself that the apparent trust he put in her stemmed from genuine appreciation. He simply didn't see her as a threat, having relegated her to the category of unobtrusive domestic help. The invisibility of service was a source of eternal fascination to her. This viewing point offered an uncompromising insight into the lives that she so easily entered. Her clients thought nothing of laying their existence bare before a total stranger, on the premise that money exchanging hands could somehow buy her blindness. Adam headed out of the front door, cigarette at the ready. His muffled voice was barely audible from inside – he must have been on the phone.

With Adam suitably distracted, Lucia decided to take her chances and venture upstairs. Now her engagement was secure, she had the ideal excuse to roam the place at her leisure. There was plenty of wallpaper to steam off, as well as old plastering to survey, and so no room was out of bounds. As she braved the lofty staircase, she noticed the dust had settled thickly on the bannister. She would start with the Professor's inner sanctum – the library. It felt like opening a secret door into another world. Despite the recent warm weather, the windows were firmly shut, leaving no escape for the smell of dry paper and overheated leather. Lucia made a superhuman effort not to sneeze.

The room was unchanged since her meeting with Professor Kiseleva. The desk was cluttered with old lecture notes, drafts of articles and what appeared to be an indiscriminate choice of books on a variety of areas of mathematics. The Professor seemed to move from one idea to the next until she narrowed in on her subject. The latest notes were on her draft book, a comparative study of Soviet and US research into the automation of decision-making. Dropping maths at the first opportunity at school had left Lucia's scientific knowledge embarrassingly lacking, a fact she now regretted. None of the content made much sense. Drafts upon drafts of the same chapters were covered in indecipherable red scribbles, like the remains of moribund insects that had crawled across the page to their death.

As much as Lucia would have wanted to linger in the library, she was conscious that time was of the essence. She closed the doors slowly behind her and set upon deciding where to go next. The other doors down the long corridors either side of the landing were all identical. One was slightly open, and this distinguishing feature made it the next port of call. It was Mrs Byrne's room. She had left her own window open, though the still air outside hadn't managed to chase away the faint smell of washing powder and recently vacuumed carpet. The housekeeper was markedly more fastidious about her personal space than she was about the rest of the house. The décor was in line with expectations – a nun's cell devoid of personality. The single bed was in the meagre company of a chest of drawers, a narrow standalone wardrobe and a single armchair covered with a well-worn throw. Lucia was momentarily held back by instinctive politeness, instantly overridden. The imminent violation had strong mitigating circumstances.

The wardrobe contained nothing but featureless, much washed clothes of the type that Mrs Byrne customarily wore. On top of the chest of drawers was a lumpen crucifix bearing the inscription "Rome, Anno Domini 2012" on the back, and, next to it, a framed photograph of an attractive auburn-haired woman holding a small boy on her lap against the background of a funfair. The unbridled joy on their faces stood in sharp contrast to the gloomy surroundings in which their fleeting impression now found itself.

Lucia thought she heard steps downstairs. The interviews were probably over. She risked one last incursion. However, the door she opened was a neatly made-up spare bedroom – nothing of note. She tried again, and this time it was Adam's room that she found herself in. It made sense why she thought the door had stuck. The floor was invisible – dirty clothes, plates and glasses were strewn liberally all around. The smell matched the montage. What Adam had been up to left little to the imagination. There were a couple of empty bottles of red wine by the bed, and a half-drunk bottle of blended whisky on the windowsill. Quite a lot more time than Lucia had at her disposal would be needed to wade through the mess. She walked downstairs with a firm but relaxed step, a simple justification at the ready, should she be challenged.

Carliss stood at the bottom of the staircase, waiting. 'I'm not even going to ask what you've been up to.' His smile indicated there would probably be no recrimination for her actions. 'Come on, let's get out of here. I could do with a pint.'

Chapter 12

Aside from the Red Lion, the other pub in the near vicinity was the wincingly named Hampstead Belle. Its unsuspecting predecessor, the Plough, had been stripped of its unsuitably low beams and rough wood floors, which had been deemed unfit to accommodate the fragile heads and designer footwear of the local clientele. The end result was a desolate open-plan hall that would have been adequate for low-budget business conferences. It was, moreover, a gastropub, serving the full range of goods available for delivery by the lorry every Monday morning. The advantage was that nobody Lucia knew drank there, especially not in the middle of a working day. Without the need for prompting, Carliss hunted down his usual pint of best bitter and a large glass of white Burgundy for his companion.

'Regale me with your exploits. How many skeletons did you find upstairs?'

'Not as many as I was hoping. I didn't get to spend much time in the bedrooms, as I didn't want to attract too much attention to my whereabouts.'

Carliss listened carefully while Lucia set out her findings, all the while adding new detail to his intricate diagram.

'Hard to believe the housekeeper was once young and pretty,' he said. 'I wonder what happened to the boy. Her son, I assume. She kept that one quiet – but then, I didn't ask.'

Lucia made a mental note to work on Mrs Byrne for this information. 'What did she have to say about the tin of poison?'

'She knew it was under the sink, of course. Said she barely ever used it – couldn't remember when she last had. She wasn't aware of anyone else tampering with it, though she couldn't be sure. On the day of the party, she prepared all the food and laid out the spread upstairs. Emilia helped. Mrs Byrne was backwards and forwards between kitchen and terrace, and once the guests arrived, she was busy attending to them. She served them drinks, and some of them – Adam in particular – also helped themselves. She didn't notice anything unusual or untoward.'

'What about the argument with Adam?'

'I asked about that too. It didn't take her by surprise – either that, or she's an excellent actress. She's been trying to get him off the drink. Every time, he swears to her on everything he holds dear that he'll give it up, only to have another relapse. That day they had a bust-up. Do you believe her?'

'It sounds plausible enough. Like I said, I couldn't hear what they were saying. She's not exactly a fan of boozing, from what I've noticed. I can't help feeling there might be more to their relationship than she's letting on, but it's just a hunch, and hunches are worth nothing without hard facts.'

'Once a lawyer, always a lawyer. OK, on to Adam.' Carliss consulted his weighty notebook. 'Adam, Adam, Adam.'

'Come on, spit it out.'

'This one's very good. Adam isn't who we thought he was.'

'You mean he's not related to the Professor?' It had been apparent all along that, whoever Adam was, he wasn't cast in the same mould as Alla Kiseleva, and it was unlikely she would have warmed to the family of a maligned husband.

If Carliss was piqued, he didn't show it. If anything, he was admirative. 'I should have known you'd work it out. OK, so who do you think he is?'

'I can't be sure of the details, but he must be connected to someone she was very fond of.'

'You're far too good at this game. He's the son of an old friend of hers, a colleague from the Mathematical Society. Martha Corcoran died prematurely – an aggressive cancer – when Adam was barely out of his teens. Adam never knew his father, so Professor Kiseleva took him in, and he's lived with her ever since.' The Detective Chief Inspector leaned back enigmatically into his chair.

Lucia could see he had a final trick up his sleeve. 'What is it now?'

'Now the Professor's gone, there's an awful lot left behind,' he said cryptically.

'You mean her will. Adam is the main beneficiary and the executor. He gets the house, and the Mathematical Society gets her money.'

Lucia had a pang of remorse at taking the wind out of Carliss's sails yet again. They had developed an ongoing game of amicable competition which they both enjoyed, all the more as neither took offence at the other's winning a round. They made a good partnership. Lucia liked the DCI's straightforwardness. With him, what you saw was what you got – a safe pair of hands, not easily fazed.

'You can do my job for me. I could go back to the station, and nobody would notice the newly promoted DCI Steer has taken over.' There was no hint of malice or bitterness in his voice. He was simply acknowledging that she had scored another point.

They laughed, a brief but necessary antidote to the unhappiness that the Professor seemed to have cultivated around her. It had been a long and intense day, and they were both ready to stop. While they were engrossed in conversation, the pub had gradually filled up with a trickle of weary commuters, reluctant to finish their return journey to lonely bedsits or demanding family homes. Lucia and DCI Carliss willed themselves to persevere for a little while longer.

'The Professor was very attached to that Society of hers. Adam's been well looked after, but if I were in the housekeeper's shoes, I'd be pretty hacked off. All those years of service and not a penny out of the estate,' said the policeman.

Lucia corrected him. 'If Mrs Byrne knew about the will, that is. She could have been entirely in the dark. And judging by what I saw in Bloomsbury, I'm not surprised the Professor endowed her brainchild so generously. Her work was her life.'

'Adam must have hoped for some cold hard cash out of the old lady, if, as you say, he's got money worries. Though I don't get why he's so desperate.' Carliss scratched his head and leafed through his notes. 'Ah, here it is. He's an accountant. Works for a firm called Runciman Parry, just behind Leadenhall Market. He can't be poor.'

'Drinking is an expensive habit.'

'Not that expensive. He wasn't paying rent, for a start.'

'Good point. Now the Professor is out of the way, he wants to shift Beatrice Hall as fast as he can. He told me to carry on with the decorating. With the current state of the property market, he's going to be a multimillionaire overnight. Paying me a few thousand to tart up the place ready for viewings is small change compared to what's about to land in his lap.'

'So, he's got a very strong motive. He bumps her off, and bang – he gets the house, so he can get on with solving his pressing cashflow issues.' Carliss paused pensively. 'He corroborated the housekeeper's story on the argument you heard in the kitchen – said she's forever on his back to clean himself up. On the poison, he says he didn't know it was there. He claims he's never looked under the kitchen sink – he would have had no reason to. He came down to the garden around three forty-five, just before the Professor, as he wanted first dibs on the champagne. Again, he says he didn't notice anything of interest.'

Lucia turned the information over in her mind. Why did it seem all too convenient? So far, they had an impossible murder and two potential motives, mitigated by some tenable explanations. The picture was incomplete.

True to form, Carliss pre-empted her. 'We're not getting very far, are we? The Professor really had a knack for angering everyone around her. But that doesn't automatically make them cold-blooded killers.' He yawned, and Lucia agreed that they had reached a natural end for the time being. 'Seeing how we're not going to solve our puzzle tonight, shall we have another one? My round again. My mum's brought me up right – I shouldn't let a lady pay for drinks.'

'In that case, I won't let that good upbringing go to waste.'

The pub was emptying now that the reluctant commuters were grudgingly making their way back to their abodes. There was nothing waiting for her at home – no pet, no children, no lover. Faced with the silence of the flat and the weight of her own imagination, Lucia far preferred the current status quo and whatever else it may bring. She was enjoying the thrill of the chase.

They went their respective ways after the second drink. Lucia ambled slowly back to Beatrice Hall, where her van was still parked. She had no compunction about getting behind the wheel following the best part of a bottle of wine. She was a confident – if somewhat reckless – driver.

As the vehicle came closer and closer into sight, she noticed something was very wrong. She stood by it for a good few minutes, hypnotised by the words that had been menacingly scrawled in tall, blood-red capitals on its side: "BITCH. YOU'LL PAY".

Chapter 13

More than anything, the defacement of her beloved van made Lucia angry. She refused to indulge in feeling sorry for herself. Instilling fear was the end goal of the vandalism, and she was damned if she was going to succumb to it. First things first. She didn't want to drive back to her place with the vehicle in that state. After taking a photo of the damage, she got out a pot of metal paint that matched the body most closely and swept over the writing. She knew it was unlikely the perpetrator would be caught, and she wasn't planning to report the incident to the police. It would have been a waste of their time, and in any case, it would have only been summarily logged and relegated to the bottom of the pile. Now it was invisible, the effect of the threat was diminished. Nonetheless, it wouldn't be wise to forget that someone out there not only wished her ill but was prepared to make it happen. She had her strong suspicions about who that someone might be.

There was no question of moping around at home passing time. Despite her best efforts to shake it off, the incident had unnerved her. She was on her own, and whoever did this must have known that. She decided a walk on the Heath would help clear her mind. The early evening sun waved in and out of soft clouds, and once she got past the first couple of ponds the grassy expanse stretched out before her, far removed from the urban clutter of Belsize Park that she had just left behind.

In the first pond past South End Green, the swan nest was empty, and the parents were proudly parading their nearly grown offspring, now improbably large but still in possession of downy grey feathers staining the immaculate white. It had been a long and dry summer, and the grass was spattered with singed patches of yellow where the worst damage had been done. A flock of feral parakeets, a semi-mythical apparition that clashed with the Englishness of the hilltop village, had settled in a tall, gnarled oak tree, their shrieks competing with the dozens of mewling prams on their final outing of the day.

Lucia had her eyes on the prize – the viewing point at Parliament Hill, from where the city could be surveyed in all its disorderly, overbuilt glory. The most distinctive landmark was St Paul's, a tiny sugary fancy of a building that somehow managed to hold its own in the midst of unforgiving glass towers. The walk had the desired palliative effect, even though she wasn't predisposed to bouts of sentimentality. The meandering circuit back to her flat would take her up to Christ Church, where she could reminisce about the familiar school playground and time whiled away at the gate before sauntering home just around the corner. Paradise twice over, her mother used to call it – four solid walls in God's own London village. That night, she couldn't sleep.

The following day, DCI Carliss smoked a stealthy cigarette as he waited for Lucia outside Beatrice Hall. He stubbed out the offending item just as she pulled up.

'What's happened to your van?'

'Oh, it's nothing. Probably bored teenagers having a dare.' As soon as she opened her mouth, she instantly knew the reply had been too quick, too dismissive to fool him.

'Nonsense. What happened?'

There was little point in carrying on with the pretence, so she decided to come clean. 'Someone – I've got a good idea who it is – wrote a nasty message in big red letters. Must have been while we were at the pub yesterday. Childish, really.' She showed him what she had found and told him about Danny.

Carliss's expression hardened. His eyes were ice-cold, his easy-going manner long gone. 'This isn't a joke, Lucia.' He'd dropped the politeness, so she knew he wasn't fooling around. 'You could be in danger. This Danny bloke sounds like a nasty piece of work. Tell you what. I'll get one of my boys to keep an eye on him, low-profile, from a distance. There's little chance we can prove anything, but people like that aren't smart enough to hide their behaviour for long. Who knows what else he's been up to?'

'Really, there's no need. I'm not scared of the likes of him.' That wasn't entirely true, and she clearly wasn't fooling the policeman.

'No ifs, no buts. It's no trouble, so it would be silly not to. I'll call the station right now, before we get distracted by the big house circus.' A short conversation ensued, with Carliss giving polite but firm instructions. 'It's all set up. We'll hear back at the end of the day. He's a sharp one, PC Harding – angling to move to CID – he won't miss a thing.'

Lucia unloaded the tools and paints out of her van. She planned on devoting the morning to her work, after which her schedule would take an entirely different turn. They went through to the drawing room, which had unwittingly metamorphosed into their de facto command centre.

Uncharacteristically, DCI Carliss had brought along a rucksack, which Lucia now eyed up intently.

'I've got a little present for you.' He fished out the Baccarat coupe, neatly packaged up in what looked like a sandwich bag, albeit extensively labelled, and handed her a pair of surgical gloves. 'What are we looking for?'

'I don't know. Something that's hiding in plain sight.'

Lucia put on the gloves and held the delicate object up to the light. Its apparent simplicity belied the painstaking craftsmanship that had been expended on the piece. There was a small amount of dried-up sticky residue at the bottom, as expected, but nothing else out of place. She ran her finger along the rim and paused for a few seconds, weighing up a thought.

'I'm fairly sure the champagne in this glass was poisoned,' she said, 'and the Professor drank it.'

Carliss was running out of patience, but Lucia rather liked seeing him squirm. She would enlighten him in good time. 'The suspense is killing me. How?'

'I'm not absolutely certain yet. I'll need to do a bit of research to confirm my theory. I don't want to toss around unsubstantiated claims.'

'OK, if you say so.' He sighed and suddenly looked very tired. 'Assuming you're right, on whatever basis, we've got our means. The killer slipped the 1080 in the Professor's cup, she drank it and collapsed. We've made a scrap of progress, theoretically speaking.' He looked around him. 'Since I haven't yet spoken to the other witnesses, I'm running out of excuses to hang around here. I thought I'd have a thorough look at the kitchen before I shoot off back to the station. What are your plans for today? You look like you're cooking something up.'

'I am. I checked out Adam's employer. They're forensic accountants, specialising in fraud investigations. I was planning to do a recce of their offices and see if I can glean any information about what exactly he does for them.' There was nothing more enticing than a spot of fieldwork, just like old times.

'Sounds like a good day out. OK, let's keep in touch and see where we get to.'

Chapter 14

Most of the morning passed by in a haze. Lucia managed to scrape down a few walls in the music room. Their bareness emphasised the stained-glass bay windows in all their florid Pre-Raphaelite glory. She wondered whether the room might look best pared back – off-white walls, so as not to compete. There was no chance she could concentrate any longer. She went back to her van, away from prying ears.

'Good morning, Runciman Parry. How can I help you?' The voice on the other end of the line was young, female, with a well-spoken but indisputable London accent.

'Good morning. Your firm was recommended to me – more precisely, Adam Corcoran, one of your accountants. Do you know if he's taking on any new clients?'

The voice paused for slightly too long. 'I'm sorry, nobody of that name works here. I can put you through to the managing partner, who I'm sure would be delighted to help.'

'No, thank you, it was Adam in particular that I wanted. Not to worry, perhaps I got his details wrong. Thank you for your time.'

Lucia felt victorious to have her supposition confirmed. If Adam had ever worked for Runciman Parry – and the receptionist's hesitation suggested this may have been the case – he no longer did. Not very clever of him to lie to the police, she mused. However, unless they had reason to disbelieve him, it was unlikely they would have followed up to check. She glanced at the dashboard clock. It would take the best part of an hour to get to Leadenhall Market. If she set off now, she would arrive in time to catch the office workers filtering out for their lunch break. There was nothing to lose.

The Northern Line took her to Bank. She walked along Cornhill, past the magisterial beauty of Tite's Royal Exchange and through the medieval heart of the City. Next came Gracechurch Street, a thinly disguised pretext to cut across the kaleidoscopic Leadenhall Market before she would finally turn into Lime Street. There, Runciman Parry inhabited an understated Art Deco block overshadowed by the outmoded futurism of the Lloyd's building. The route was satisfyingly deserted – the mobs had not yet been released for their allocated hour-long reprieve. Every other doorway was a bar, pub, or restaurant, with smartly dressed waiters and conservative menus to accommodate the tastes of the few professions that maintained their dedication to the disappearing art of client entertainment. Lawyers and bankers had long given up the luxury of a liquid lunch and had cornered themselves into bland, hypoallergenic meals washed down with still water in meeting rooms. Insurance was the only industry left to resolutely fly the flag for brightly coloured socks and sybaritic occasions lubricated with rivers of claret. The market was their stomping ground, where deals were sealed over lunchtime pints and afternoons were spent reluctantly sobering up before doing it all again in the evening.

On Lime Street, the neat row of brass plates at the main entrance bore evidence that the address housed a number of businesses. Lucia paced up and down on the pavement outside, struggling to conjure up a new strategy. When she lifted her head, she couldn't believe her luck. Through the ground floor windows she glimpsed a reception desk inscribed with the unadventurous but assertive Runciman Parry logo. Behind it sat the neatly attired spitting image of the barmaid at the Red Lion. This had to be her girl. On the dot of one, the receptionist sprang to her feet, grabbed her large, soft-leathered handbag, outward proof that the firm was generous with its remuneration, and strode out of the door. She was wearing a pencil dress and vertiginous heels better suited to a photo shoot than the uneven cobbles that they were forced to negotiate. Lucia followed closely behind her. The girl walked into the nearest sandwich shop and joined the mercifully short queue. She soon settled at a table and pulled out her phone.

Over the years, Lucia had narrowed down her investigative techniques to the two that elicited the most results – cajoling and directness. The present situation called for the latter. She walked over and sat down at the receptionist's table. The girl looked up for a moment and instantly retreated back to her phone. It was a busy lunchtime, after all, and there were no other seats left.

'Hi. It's Gemma, isn't it? You work at Runciman Parry.' As with the handbag, Lucia had deduced that outward presentation was key. The receptionist had ensured that her career progression was widely advertised on all public channels.

She had got the girl's attention. The manicured hands clutched the phone tightly, but the thickly feathered cat eyes glanced up.

'Yeah. Who are you?'

'I'm a friend of Adam Corcoran's. I'm sorry to come up to you like this, but I'm worried. We all are. He's been acting strangely – he's not sleeping, not eating, drinking himself stupid. For a while I've suspected he's out of a job, but he won't talk about it. I just want to know what's going on, so I can help.'

Gemma scrunched her face in disbelief. Before she could say anything, Lucia went on. If this didn't work, nothing would.

'Please, I really am desperate. His aunt's just passed away – they were very close – and that's made him retreat even further into his shell. I know you understand. Don't we all have a friend, a cousin, a brother, or someone who needs help but won't ask for it?'

One of the elements in the plea had hit the spot – at a guess, the brother part. Gemma thought hard. She flicked her head to one side, then back to her phone and eventually looked Lucia straight in the eye.

'Alright. They sacked him a couple of months ago. I don't know what came over him. He was one of the well-behaved, quiet types, you know, always polite to us girls, buying everyone drinks after work on a Friday. A few weeks before they let him go, he changed. He was in late, left early, hardly spent any time at his desk. Always popping out "for coffee," he said. The day he got sent home was a train crash. He shouted at a client and stormed out in the middle of a meeting. He was in a bad way, practically foaming at the mouth. They told him not to bother coming back.'

'Did you ever speak to him? Did he hint at what may be wrong?'

'No. Not for want of trying, mind you. He always put on a brave face and said he was fine. I'm guessing that's what he does at home, too.' Gemma looked genuinely concerned.

'Yes, just like at home. Thanks, Gemma. You don't know what a great help you've been.'

'I hope he cleans himself up. He's a good bloke, just lost his way.'

She had a soft spot for him, that much was obvious. In films, naïve girls always fell for cold-blooded killers, Lucia thought. She reminded herself she hadn't yet proved he was in that category.

She debated whether to call Carliss straightaway and decided against it. He was probably poring over the remaining witness statements, and there was no point in distracting him. Besides, she thought she should get back to Beatrice Hall and settle into her work, lest Adam might think she was slacking off. It really was the perfect cover for gathering further intelligence on the suspects. She was incorrigible.

Chapter 15

The walk back to Bank had been marred by a downpour that no longer dried as soon as it hit the ground. By the time Lucia emerged shivering into the daylight at Belsize Park, the rain had given way to unabated sunshine, and she warmed up a little in her damp clothes. Haverstock Hill was liberally sprinkled with the familiar mid-afternoon clientele – mothers and maternal substitutes carting around varyingly sized children, elderly ladies lugging mysterious packages to the post office and builders enjoying surreptitious cans of Red Bull. Nobody had anything urgent to do, nowhere pressing to be. The wheels of this corner of affluent North London, well-oiled by an army of absent City workers, turned slowly.

Lucia let herself in – Adam had thankfully entrusted her with a key, so she could come and go as she liked, without owing an explanation – and headed straight down to the kitchen. She half hoped she might bump into Mrs Byrne, although she would have preferred the interlude of a solitary cup of tea first. Her wish was granted. She couldn't resist checking under the sink. The unexceptional selection of cleaning products matched what she had expected to find. Once she had had her few minutes of peace, she wondered where the housekeeper might be. A sudden clatter of what sounded like metal on metal interrupted the solitude. It was coming from the direction of the back garden. Aside from the tea party, Lucia realised she had never seen Mrs Byrne out of the semi-obscurity of the house.

The French doors in the drawing room were wide open, just like they had been on that day. The garden was large for London, although at least a third of it was paved. Scrawny weeds had shot up in between the worn-down slabs, comfortable in the knowledge that they would not be disturbed. The lawn was hay-like, having evidently lost a fair few battles with the sun. Despite the maturity of the plants, the borders were straggly and unkempt, a mixture of neglected long-timers and accidental growth. At the bottom of the garden, Mrs Byrne was busy hacking away at a patch of unsuspecting dahlias, now withered to a crisp, that would have happily provided a final taste of summer had they been regularly deadheaded. Adam must have been trying to save himself a few pennies on the gardening. At the rate the housekeeper was going, the costs of remedying the carnage stood to overtake any savings made.

'Hello, Mrs Byrne. Do you want a hand with that?'

The woman jumped, as if she had just been caught in a compromising situation. 'Lucia. Hello, love, I didn't see you there. I'm alright, thanks. Been doing this for years. Nice to see you. You've been busy, I take it.'

Lucia sensed Mrs Byrne welcomed the interruption.

'Yes, it's not too bad. It's the wallpaper that's giving me the most trouble. Layers and layers of it, all on top of each other. That's how things were done, before these new-fangled steamers we've got now.'

Mrs Byrne's huffing and puffing was somewhat out of proportion to the light task in hand. 'Oh, I'm done in. I've been at this garden all day.' Given the time allegedly expended, the progress on the ground was fairly light.

'Why don't I take a break? I'm gasping for a cuppa, and I bet you are too.'

'I'd love one, Mrs Byrne.' Lucia was determined to drink as much tea as was necessary to shake down her prey.

After a good ten minutes, the housekeeper returned, weighed down with mugs. 'No harm in sitting ourselves down for a moment or two.'

They went over to the wrought iron table, which Lucia assumed – indeed hoped – must have been wiped down since it housed the food and drink for the party. The chairs must have been expensive when bought, but the padding had worn down, and they were now downright uncomfortable, like most of the furniture in the house.

'That's better.' The housekeeper took a noisy mouthful of the brew and sighed, wallowing pleasantly in her minor martyrdom. 'I'm too old for this backbreaking work. Adam won't get a gardener in. Says we can't afford such luxuries now… now that she's gone.'

There it was again – the guilt and, judging by the almost imperceptible tremor in her voice, a touch of fear.

'You must really miss her. You were with her for so long.' Lucia's tone was sympathetic, undemanding. With the right nudge, she was optimistic that Mrs Byrne would open up.

Mrs Byrne paused, stumped for words. She searched for the appropriate response, as she didn't seem to miss the Professor at all. 'Yes. I have been here an awfully long time. I've given my best years to this place – to her. It's strange now that she's gone.' Since she could not think of anything substantive to contribute, she was repeating herself.

Lucia tried a different route in. 'You've done a wonderful job. And all on your own.'

Her companion's expression shifted to coy. 'Hmm, yes. It's a big old house.' She paused, unsure whether to carry on. Lucia looked out admiringly onto the garden. 'It was a lot easier when I had Connor to help me.' There, she'd said it. Her eyes welled up. She shook her head. 'Pesky hay fever. You'd think it would be over by now. I bet it's the pollution. All these huge cars everyone drives nowadays.'

Lucia didn't want to lose her now, but knew she had to stay put. It was important to maintain an air of non-committed interest – any further probing, and Mrs Byrne would have got spooked.

Sure enough, the tactic worked. 'Connor was my son, you see.'

At this point, Lucia calculated that some light, direct questioning would be appropriate.

'Did he work for the Professor too?'

'He did.' Mrs Byrne's expression darkened, but she was too far down the line to put a halt to her involuntary confession. 'Until she let him go, that is. Oh, I don't know why I'm bringing this up now. It feels good to talk to someone about it, you know. Ever since that woman died, it's been police here, there, and everywhere, asking me about the food, the drink, where I made it, where I put it, what the guests were doing. Nobody asked about me. Nobody cared how I felt.'

Lucia thought the housekeeper was doing incredibly well not to cry but realised that over time, the sadness had been insidiously replaced with animosity. Mrs Byrne had no tears left to mourn for her son.

'I do, Mrs Byrne. I care how you feel. And I want to listen.'

By this point, Mrs Byrne wouldn't have noticed anything that came from Lucia. She was absolutely determined to get matters off her chest. 'Poor boy. He didn't have a father, you see – Michael died when he was little. Connor was ever so good with his hands, and such a gentle lad. Ever since he could walk, he was always following me around, doing what I was doing, wanting to help. He knew it was just the two of us. It wasn't his fault he started drinking, his father had been the same. I tried so hard to get him to stop, and he was getting better, said he hadn't touched a drop in weeks. And then the Professor goes and gives him the boot.'

So much anger, hidden deep down inside for so long. Lucia felt genuine regret for prizing this knowledge out of Mrs Byrne, but it had to be done.

'She said she'd had enough of seeing him stumble around, blind-drunk. She couldn't trust him, she said. And just like that, my boy was gone.' Mrs Byrne fixed Lucia with blazing eyes. 'The next time I saw him was when they fished him out of Camden Lock. I had to identify the body. It's all that woman's doing. She killed my son.'

It had taken extraordinary strength to reach the end of her speech. The housekeeper sat back in her chair, drained.

'I'm sorry. I can't even begin to imagine what you've been through. Connor was very lucky to have a mother like you.'

Mrs Byrne smiled a little. She must have rehearsed this story dozens of times in her head, but it was no less painful. She returned to her tea. 'He was a good boy, my Connor. Fixed everything around the house, and never once answered back. But that wasn't good enough for her ladyship in the end. Just not good enough.'

There was solace to be found in the Professor's demise. The story gave the housekeeper a conceivable motive.

Hand in hand with absolution came embarrassment. 'Look at me sitting here feeling sorry for myself. What's done is done. You can't hold a grudge against the dead.' Mrs Byrne definitely looked like she could. 'Didn't mean to be so glum, child. Don't let me hold you any longer. Those flowers need seeing to.' She trotted off back to the defenceless dahlias.

Lucia took the mugs back into the house. Much had been achieved. It was time to give Carliss a call.

'Hi, Lucia. I'm down at the station. Do you mind coming here? I'm not quite done yet.'

Chapter 16

Kentish Town Police Station had all the attributes of the average public institution – ample late Victorian frontage, engraved round-arched entrance and late twentieth-century additions that Richard Norman Shaw would have frowned upon. The only indulgence was the spindly palm tree guarding the steps up to the door, which lent an air of dissonant frivolity to an otherwise perfectly functional construction. Lucia presented herself at the front counter and asked for DCI Carliss.

'I've never been inside a police station,' she remarked.

'You haven't missed much. They're all the same. For reasons I won't bore you with, my team's only been here a short while. At least this place looks nice on the outside. Inside, it's all flimsy partitions and false ceilings. The view isn't particularly thrilling either.'

Carliss's office looked precisely as billed. His desk was scrupulously tidy and devoid of any personal items. No framed certificates marked the bare walls. The public sector had enthusiastically adopted the paper-free edict and obeyed it religiously, if his room was anything to go by.

They sat across from each other, separated by the desk. Carliss was uncharacteristically quiet. Lucia decided she would go first.

'I've had a very productive day.'

'I bet you had.' He sounded fed up, like he had run out of steam.

'I paid a visit to the forensic accountants. Our boy Adam is out of a job. They sacked him for erratic behaviour, which tallies with his drinking. That would explain the money worries.'

The inspector perked up a little. Perhaps his day had been dull in comparison. 'That's good. I don't mean for him. It confirms his motive. He was in dire need of cash. Don't tell me how you found out. I get the feeling that, with you, some things are best kept under wraps.'

Lucia wasn't certain whether or not he was joking but resolved to act as if he did. 'Nothing fruity, don't worry. Just made friends with the receptionist. You'd be amazed what you can find out, if only you dare ask.'

'So far I like him for it. In any case, never mind he's got motive, we don't even know how the poison got into the Professor's system. For now, at least, it's all moot.'

It all fell into place. He was angry with her for not sharing how the Professor had been killed. She hadn't realised that holding on to this piece of information had affected him so much. It was high time she put things right. 'I haven't told you yet because I wasn't sure myself. Now I am.'

He listened keenly as she expounded her theory. When she was done, he leaned back in his chair, his face coloured by surprise and relief. 'And you're sure of this?'

'As sure as I can be without actually having witnessed the event. I've run a test, and it works.'

Now that bridges had been mended, Lucia recounted her get-together with Mrs Byrne. 'Heart-breaking stuff,' she concluded. 'Mrs Byrne isn't exactly highly qualified, so she stayed on. She blames her employer for her son's death, that much is clear. That's arguably motive. But why now? Why not kill her at any point after Connor died?'

DCI Carliss considered this latest revelation. 'You know what they say – revenge is a dish best served cold. Maybe the poor woman just couldn't take any more and snapped. Or maybe she was more calculated than that and waited until the ideal opportunity presented itself.'

'Maybe.'

'You don't sound like you buy it.'

'Not entirely. It doesn't quite fit. Mrs Byrne doesn't strike me as the calculating type. She can certainly hold a grudge, we know that, but if she were to take any action, it would be, as you say, because she can't bear the pain any longer. That would lead her to commit a violent, unplanned act – hitting the Professor over the head, stabbing her with a kitchen knife – which she would then go to great lengths to cover up.'

'Perhaps.'

'Now *you* don't sound convinced.'

'I don't think we should rule her out just yet. In my professional experience, a mother blaming someone for her child's death doesn't herself know what she's capable of.'

The telephone on the desk interrupted them with a metallic screech. 'Carliss. Yes. PC Harding.' He got Lucia's attention with a flick of the eyelids. 'OK. Thanks. Make sure you stay on his tail tomorrow, and the day after, until we get something on him.'

'Nothing on Danny then?' Lucia was convinced they were wasting their time. With no CCTV or witnesses, it would be nigh on impossible to prove he was responsible for vandalising her van.

'Nothing as yet. Danny arrived for his job just after eight this morning. A flat on Flask Walk. He left on his own at four and drove to the builders' merchant in Colindale, then went home to Rhyl Street. Something's telling me not to give up. Call it instinct, or experience.'

'It's your call. I honestly don't care about the van. It's easy enough to fix.' They both knew this was a futile protest. Despite her stubbornness, Lucia was flattered that someone should want to look out for her. She had been on her own for so long that she had forgotten how to rely on others. She didn't want to ever depend on another person if she could help it. But there was an undeniable feeling of contentment in knowing that he cared.

The inspector raised an eyebrow. Lucia sensed he wasn't at ease – the confusing soup of motives and hidden feelings thrown up by the Professor's death was evidently perplexing him. He scoured through his encyclopaedic notebook. 'I've heard back from my people in the Home Office.'

Lucia piped up. 'Oh, yes. And?'

'Nothing. From what they've got sight of, there's no trace of Professor Alla Kiseleva in Russia. Beyond what we know already through the standard police channels, she's got no ascertainable past in her home country.'

This was regrettable. They had harboured high hopes of finding something new. Lucia wondered whether there was another channel that might yield better results. She had relatively unfettered access to it, although she held back from employing it unless strictly necessary. The current situation most definitely called for it.

'Slippery character indeed.' She looked around his bare office. 'Not one for interior design, then?'

'Not at work. I like to keep my personal taste private. Work is just where I go to – well – do work. It doesn't need to be cosy. I'm calling it a day. Drink?'

'Not tonight, thanks. I need to sleep off all this excitement.' Lucia knew full well she wouldn't sleep but felt a duty to at least try.

'Alright then. I'm off to the depths of East London tomorrow to check up on Emilia Poole. I'll keep you posted,' said the policeman.

Lucia recalled Emilia's symmetrical face and wondered what Detective Chief Inspector Carliss would make of her.

Chapter 17

East London was, as far as DCI David Carliss was concerned, a different country. Just as he was acutely conscious of crossing the Thames to travel south, the world that lay beyond the A1 was to be approached with heightened caution. Upper Street was the second last bastion of North London gentility, if the enclave of De Beauvoir Town was to be – rather generously, he thought – categorised as the last. Once you crossed the A10, all bets were off. He heartened himself that Hackney and Shoreditch had been subjected to an intensive programme of gentrification, as evidenced by the upscale farmers' markets and attentively curated outfits that filled the *Evening Standard*. This led him to wonder how Emilia Poole could afford to live there. He finished his coffee and checked the address again. He took an old-fashioned approach to navigation, preferring to avoid street view maps – he viewed them as tantamount to cheating, or at the very least conducive to unnecessary prejudices.

The forgiving temperatures of mid-September had given way to the inescapable decline into low-lit melancholy that would not lift until the middle of spring. The pavement was pockmarked by a light drizzle, and the city looked in its element. The sultriness that other European capitals wore so well didn't suit London. The natural habitat of Bethnal Green tube station was largely in line with expectations – sanitized chain cafes, down-at-heel neighbourhood businesses and self-consciously hip pubs. The address was a slim, grubby doorway beside a phone unlocking shop. There were three buzzers – how three flats could fit in the allocated space was unfathomable. No doubt C was a crow's nest perched on top of the building and invisible from the road, the kind that would be uninhabitable in temperatures above twenty degrees. Emilia's flat was B.

'Come on in.' Her voice was more high-pitched than he had imagined – he barely remembered her from the tea party. He climbed up the stairs and tried not to breathe in too deeply. The amalgamation of stale cooking odours and old carpet nearly made him retch. The door inscribed with B was wide open. He knocked out of generic politeness, walked in and shut it behind him.

Compared with the dinginess of the communal area, the flat was spotlessly clean. It was adequately furnished, but there was no question of the place being anything other than digs. Emilia sat on the low sofa, hands crossed in her lap.

'Good morning, Miss Poole. Detective Chief Inspector David Carliss of the Metropolitan Police.'

'Good morning, Inspector. Won't you please sit down? And can I offer you a drink?' She gestured to a dining chair that had been placed opposite her for this purpose.

His memory was jolted. Together with Lucia's depiction, he had now formed a clear image of her. Her fair hair, neatly scraped back, was naturally blonde – not the Scandinavian variety, but a richer, golden shade of a less recurrent kind. The bareness of her face accentuated her earnest brown eyes. The presentation had the disconcerting effect of an open book. For all his preparation, Carliss found himself at a loss where to start.

'No, thank you, I've just had a coffee. Thank you for making the time to see me. The statement you gave my colleagues was very comprehensive. There are only a few outstanding points I'd like to address, so it shouldn't take too long.'

'Of course. I'd be very happy to help.' Emilia smiled, as diligent as can be. She was wearing a high-necked black dress, expertly draped, that left less to the imagination than a low-cut equivalent would have done. The policeman's eyes wandered to parts of her anatomy that were not relevant to a formal encounter.

'First, can you tell me a little about yourself? How did you come to work for Professor Kiseleva?'

Emilia tilted her head to one side and sighed. The statement had already covered all this ground, but Carliss wanted to get a direct sense of whom he was faced with.

'I started as her personal assistant eighteen months ago. The job was posted on an academic website and involved research and proofreading. It matched my skills, and I was hired.'

'Did you have previous experience in this line of work?'

'I used to be a teacher. English at St Wenna's.' The inspector recognized the name – it was a well-known girls' private school in West London.

'If you don't mind me asking, Miss Poole, why did you leave teaching to be a personal assistant? It seems an unlikely career progression.'

Evidently, it was a question she was used to being asked. The half-smile she graced him with had changed from solicitous to sardonic. 'You clearly have no idea what it's like to be a teacher.'

'Tell me. What is it like?' DCI Carliss was secretly pleased that he had broken her composure, until it occurred to him that the rendition might be well rehearsed.

'I don't mean to speak ill of my former employer, but…' She searched for the appropriate words. 'The place was run shambolically. It prided itself on its liberal ethos.

All it meant in practice was that discipline was impossible to enforce. In simple terms, Inspector, the girls were spoilt brats and there was nothing I could do about it.' The self-righteousness she affected suited her. It was a valid reason for her not to have stayed on.

'And you didn't look for another teaching job?'

'I fancied a career change.'

Carliss consulted the notes from the preliminary interview that he had conscientiously stapled in his notebook.

'You left your post at St Wenna's two years ago, and you started your job with the Professor eighteen months ago. What did you do for the six months in between?'

'Temping.'

'Temping?'

'Yes, temping. Working occasional office jobs here and there.'

He knew what temping meant but couldn't understand why anyone would want to do it. He had been in the police force since he left school.

'Isn't that a touch entry-level for a highly qualified teacher?' He had read her CV – privately educated, English at Oxford. She had been at St Wenna's since she finished her teaching qualifications and had swiftly risen to head of department. He also remembered Lucia's remark, but allowed himself to think he had been first to articulate it.

Emilia sat back into the sofa, crossed her legs, and stroked her smooth ponytail. She was undeniably the mistress of the anodyne rented flat.

'I enjoyed it. It afforded the kind of freedom that traditional employment can't offer. I have no partner, dependants or mortgage to account to, so I can do as I like.' There was a light but unmistakable note of defiance in her tone.

'Do you live alone, Miss Poole? Any family?'

He thought he caught a fleeting cloud pass across her serene face, but, if it ever existed, it was gone in a fraction of a second. 'My flatmate is an ICU nurse. She's hardly ever here and when she is, she's generally asleep. As for family, my parents died four years ago. Car accident. I'm an only child. To my knowledge, I don't have any other relatives that are alive.'

Although he was keen to dig deeper into her background, Carliss didn't feel it was directly relevant to the investigation, and thus appropriate, to continue with this particular line of questioning.

'I'm sorry to hear about your parents. I'd like to move on to the day of the party. Can you give me a brief account of your whereabouts?'

'I arrived at Beatrice Hall around nine in the morning, as I usually do. I was there all day. Apart from stretching our legs and eating a sandwich lunch in the garden, the Professor and I were in the library. She was writing a new chapter and I was reading an older draft. At three-thirty or so, the Professor went to her room to change. I went down to the kitchen to help Mrs Byrne prepare the food and drink, and we took it out onto the terrace.'

'Did you know the Professor had a recognizable champagne coupe that was different from the other glasses set out for the guests?'

'Of course. Everyone did. She always used that coupe. It had been a gift from her mother.'

Carliss was hoping to shock her into revealing something of note, though he had no idea what. 'Did you know there was a tin of rat poison kept under the kitchen sink?'

Emilia looked genuinely surprised.

'No, I had no idea. I've never looked under the sink.' Her compelling eyes widened in horror. 'Is that what killed her? Rat poison?'

'I'm not in position to say just yet. So, you went downstairs around three-thirty, set up for the party, and then what?'

It took Emilia a few moments to shake off the unpleasant recollection of the Professor's death. 'Sorry, yes. The guests started to arrive shortly before four. The Walkers were the first, I believe, if you don't count Adam, who appeared not long after we brought out the food and drink. Dr Glover arrived at four on the dot. I remember because I thought to myself how wonderfully punctual he always is. I was mingling, eating, drinking – I didn't leave the terrace – until… until the incident.' She couldn't bring herself to describe it more specifically.

Carliss noted that Emilia had omitted to mention Lucia's arrival. As the decorator herself would have said, tradespeople were generally forgotten about.

'You've been very helpful, Miss Poole, much appreciated. Just one last question, if I may. Did you notice anything out of place, anyone acting strangely during the party, or beforehand?'

After the bland responses from Adam Corcoran and Mrs Byrne, Carliss had in all honesty not expected this to be the killer question. Emilia furrowed her shapely eyebrows, deep in thought.

'Now you mention it, there was something.'

'Go on.'

'It's probably nothing, which is why it slipped my mind completely.' She was being both helpful and apologetic.

'Don't worry. It often takes some time after the event to recall snippets of information that we've filed away as unimportant. It's how the human brain works.'

'This wasn't on the day of the party. It was about a week before, though I can't be sure of the precise date. It was shortly after nine in the morning, as I'd just arrived. The Professor and I had settled in the library as usual when the doorbell rang. Shortly after, Mrs Byrne came in to say that John Walker was there to see her. The Professor went downstairs. The door was left open, and I heard what sounded like a heated discussion, albeit with lowered voices. I couldn't make out what they were saying, but I'm fairly certain it wasn't friendly. It only lasted a few minutes, and the Professor came back up. She acted as if nothing had happened. As I said, it's likely to be meaningless.'

'Perhaps, but it's a fact worth banking. Was there anyone else in the house who could have heard the row?'

'I don't think so. Adam had gone out. I heard Mrs Byrne's steps going down the stairs back to the kitchen, so she was probably out of earshot.'

'Well, thank you again for your time, Miss Poole. If anything else occurs to you, please give me a ring anytime, day or night.' He handed her a business card, which she slipped into the pocket of her fitted dress.

As he turned to leave, Emilia's phone started vibrating noisily. It was on the kitchen table, within easy reach. She scooped it up with a deft hand, but not sufficiently fast to prevent Carliss from catching a glimpse of the caller's name – Stewart Ross. She silenced it and set it aside with a dismissive glance.

They said their final, terse goodbyes at the door. Carliss decided on a detour via a greasy spoon for an imperative late breakfast. The first couple of places that could have been likely contenders had misleadingly retained the old shop windows but turned out to be serving coffee that took a good fifteen minutes to produce, despite the major role in the process being performed by a reliable Italian-manufactured machine. He was lucky on the third attempt – no calligraphed blackboard and a greasy linoleum floor patched with gaffer tape. It was time to give Lucia a ring.

Chapter 18

Lucia sat cross-legged on her bed, poring over her laptop, and surrounded by a growing pile of mugs and plates that she had been too engrossed in her train of thought to notice. A pattern of connections was gradually starting to take shape – a labyrinthine, asymmetrical spiderweb. She even managed to shut out the uniform whirr of the phone; it took Carliss three attempts before he heard her voice.

'So, there you have it,' Carliss concluded, having delivered his account of the morning's rendezvous. 'I bent over backwards to pick holes in her story, but there aren't any. The only thing I can accuse her of is being well versed in social interaction with the opposite sex.'

Lucia chuckled. The poor unsuspecting man had fallen hook, line and sinker for Emilia's wholesome charm, as she had correctly predicted he would. Nevertheless, that didn't make the woman a liar or furnish her with a motive for the murder. 'She does make for a convincing ingénue,' she said, not without a hint of jealousy.

'She mentioned her parents died in a car crash, but I didn't get a chance to probe any further,' added the inspector.

'I can fill in the gaps on that.' Lucia hadn't spent the entire morning locked up in her flat for nothing. 'Her parents are – were – Richard and Christine Poole. For years they managed a small, exclusive investment fund in Mayfair – the minimally regulated kind that looks after people who want to keep a lid on the source of their funds. Their death made the papers, on account of the theatrical backdrop: "Secretive Financiers in Ferrari Smash-up on Italian Riviera". You couldn't make it up. Their disastrous fame didn't end there. Shortly after the accident, it came to light that they had been mismanaging clients' money, dipping their hands in the cash, making reckless investments – you name it, they did it. The aftermath of litigation wiped out their entire estate. Even the serious financial publications entertained their readership with endless pictures of the enviable Chelsea house, now shamefully repossessed. There was a single mention of their daughter, an afterthought, but sufficient to confirm the link.' Lucia was in her element.

'So that explains why she lives in a grotty house share. Long way to fall, from Chelsea to Bethnal Green,' Carliss concluded. 'Which makes it all the more peculiar why she gave up her cushy teaching job.'

'You're right, it's a hell of a lifestyle change. But hear me out. Imagine you're the adored only child of wealthy parents. One day, your whole world is shattered by a freak event. Isn't it plausible that she might have been affected? Mentally, I mean.'

'You're saying she lost her marbles?'

'She wouldn't necessarily have to go as far as that. I think they call it depression these days, by the way. It's eminently treatable, but it could plausibly account for her behaviour.'

'So, she was short of money. That's not in itself a motive. I can't see how she would profit from the Professor's death.'

'Neither can I. What intrigues me is her account of the so-called argument between the Professor and John Walker. Funny she didn't mention it before – she had plenty of opportunity, and surely any abnormal occurrence involving the victim is relevant.'

'You'd be surprised what your mind blocks out following a shocking event.'

Lucia was, unsurprisingly, provoked. 'You don't actually buy it, do you? Amazing what a pair of limpid eyes and a tight dress can do to a man's judgment.' The utterance came out more dramatically than she intended. She wasn't being objective, and she knew it. 'Sorry, I'm a bit on edge. Too many hours in a confined space reading nonsense on the computer. We should check out this supposed quarrel. I've got a plan if you'll let me get on with it. Oh, and send me the Walkers' home number, please.'

'Go for it. Just don't tell me how you got your results.' This time his tone was light. 'Any idea who this Stewart Ross might be?'

'Not yet.' She did have a vague supposition, but it was not sufficiently well formed to be worth disclosing.

'Right. I've got to go. Let me know how you get on with Walker. And don't do anything stupid – by which I mean put yourself in danger.'

'I'm flattered by your concern, but I have managed to get to my venerable age without your expert assistance. See you later.' She knew he would take the comment as it was intended – in jest. She was comforted by his concern for her wellbeing, not that it would have stopped her acting recklessly if the situation so required. She dialled the Belsize Park number.

'Good afternoon, Walkers' residence. How can I help you?' Phone answering duties had evidently been relegated to the Eastern European housekeeper.

'Please could I speak to Margaret? It's Lucia Steer, the interior designer.'

After what seemed an interminable wait, Margaret's breezy voice popped up. 'Lucia. How delightful to hear from you. Yes, of course I remember. We met at the Professor's tea party. What a terrible, terrible thing. Oh, we've been so distraught. Such a lovely neighbour. What an unspeakably awful way to go.'

The use of emphatic superlatives was tiring – no doubt they sought to disguise the emptiness inside. Stop it. You're just being mean now, Lucia admonished herself. She wasn't immune from forming her own prejudices at times.

'How are you holding up? You must be so upset,' added Margaret.

'I'm not too bad, thank you. It's such a dreadful affair. I'm still working on the house, keeping myself busy. I know you mentioned you were thinking of having some work done. I'd very much like to help if that's still on the cards.'

'Of course! I didn't want to ask, what with the recent… events. The loss of someone close takes time to bed in, and I didn't want to seem – well – insensitive.'

Lucia didn't have the Professor and Margaret down as bosom buddies. The latter came across as one of those people who labelled everyone that they met a 'friend' to demonstrate the width of their social circle.

Notwithstanding the professed ordeal she had recently experienced, the minor matter of a violent death hadn't deterred Margaret from fantasizing about paint colours. 'I'm sure you're positively swamped with Beatrice Hall, but is there any chance you could squeeze us in, say, this week?'

'No problem. I can drop by in my lunchbreak tomorrow if that suits?'

'Marvellous. Johnny will be thrilled, I'm sure. It's such a drag finding good tradespeople. I can't stand all these gruff men who think they know best and then charge you double for what you didn't tell them to do.'

Perhaps Margaret wasn't so dim after all, which made the prospect of the visit all the more enticing.

Chapter 19

The work at Beatrice Hall had become cursory, a lull in the established routine of the investigation. Still, nobody seemed to mind. Lucia barely saw Adam – he rushed in and out, perpetually on his phone, or hid upstairs in his room. Since her impromptu divulgence, Mrs Byrne kept well out of the way.

The Walkers' garden abutted the Professor's, separated from each other by a wooden fence tall enough to protect the privacy of the respective households. Lucia walked around the corner and past their front door, then back again, so as to get a full view. The Walkers lived in a square, dependable mid-terrace Edwardian house. The exterior had been fairly recently restored, with the addition of a Staffordshire blue brick fence partially covered by a methodically trimmed box hedge. Lucia walked up to the door and noted the pristine front garden, with its bristly patch of lawn and orderly, well-attended planters. Margaret certainly possessed an unequivocal talent for engaging efficient staff. She opened the door with an all-encompassing smile.

'Lucia, come in. So nice to see you.'

Lucia detested public displays of affection, but in this instance decided that resistance would be both futile and ill-advised. She submitted to Margaret's double air kiss with all the polite tolerance she could muster. She was naturally suspicious of clients who were overly keen to blur the boundaries between themselves and the service provider. They were the most likely to complain profusely about the work done.

Despite her preconceptions about John and Margaret Walker, many of which she liked to think she was conscious of, Lucia felt vindicated as she entered the house. It was just as she had pictured it. There were two shades of white – one with a touch of grey for the communal areas, and one with a hint of green for the rooms. There was nothing wrong with it. Coupled with the fact that the renovation had entailed ripping out the majority of the original three-dimensional features, the overall effect was neutral and indecisive.

Hot drinks were offered and accepted. They sat on tall stools at the island in the middle of the kitchen, which happened to act as a perfect viewing platform. The housekeeper was either not present or had been sent on a conveniently timed errand.

'What do you think?'

Lucia surmised that Margaret's expectant look could not have coped with an accurate assessment.

'You have a lovely house. Very ordered.'

The route to the kitchen, which was at the back of the house and was mostly comprised of an oversized glass extension, took them past the living room and gave Lucia ample chance to pass judgment on the décor. Grey carpet, grey sofas, even grey scatter cushions, an item which Lucia violently disliked irrespective of its colour. Vapid abstract pictures – no doubt originals – peppered the walls, chosen primarily to add a limited range of colours to the otherwise blanched setting. The original fireplace had been cauterized out of existence, and its shiny showroom replacement was framed by built-in shelves lined with sparsely distributed books. The place was box-fresh and uninspiring. It suited Margaret to a tee, with her long, flawlessly blonde bob, intentionally at odds with her unfitted jeans and band T-shirt. She wanted to be Lucia's age, but must have been at least five years older, despite concerted efforts to reverse natural decline.

'You see, that's just it. Ordered. It's too ordered. Don't get me wrong, we had it done a couple of years ago and I absolutely love it. But then I saw what you did with the teal wallpaper at Beatrice Hall and it got me thinking that perhaps I haven't been very… adventurous. Or true to myself.' She hugged her mug of coffee to her chest. 'You see, deep down I'm a free spirit. I love art and colour and life… and I feel that's what we're missing here.'

Lucia queried whether a virtue-signalling outfit automatically endowed its owner with bohemian credentials. In her imagination, the harsh lines of the cruelly gutted house had already been softened with pattern and colour. She had come thoroughly prepared and produced some choice photographs of past projects where she had encountered precisely the same problem – it came with the territory. Margaret let out a range of approving noises. She desperately wanted Lucia to instruct her who she should be, and to make it happen. Personal development was one of the many tasks in her military-grade planner to be outsourced to the professionals.

'I'm impressed how you manage to keep everything so tidy, with children in tow.' Lucia had spotted a single tell-tale sign – two pairs of small squeaky-clean shoes at the entrance. The housekeeper must have had her work cut out.

'Thank you. See, that's why I think this place needs a woman's touch.' Despite falling into that category herself, Margaret didn't see it fit to perform the function. 'Johnny has no idea. He comes home from work and takes the cleanliness and tidiness for granted. He probably thinks a fairy leaps out of the cupboard at night and sprinkles her magic dust. Keeping house is a full-time job.' For someone else, evidently. 'Of course, I'm very lucky. Lily and Oscar are such well-behaved children. We struck gold with the latest nanny. You just don't know whom you're going to get these days, and where they've come from. Well, we have a few hours of peace and quiet left. They won't be back from school until half three. Kumon Maths is off today – the teacher's pulled a sickie – so it will be lovely to have them around a bit earlier than normal. Child-rearing is such hard work, but so rewarding. Being a mother is definitely my calling. Do you have children?'

Lucia had to work hard not to switch off during Margaret's waffling. Lonely, under-occupied housewives were invariably a treasure trove of information, although some effort was required to sift through it.

'I don't. I can imagine it's a lot of work.'

'Oh, it is. I'm practically a single mother. Johnny works so hard. He's barely ever home before nine, and that's if I'm lucky. I shouldn't complain. He mucks in so enthusiastically at the weekend. Last Saturday I was able to send the nanny home at midday, and he took them to see the ducks on the Heath. Such a devoted father.'

With the relentless stream of consciousness that was being fired at her, Lucia had forgotten to observe the kitchen itself. She glanced around her with an expert eye. The effect was the same as the rest of the downstairs. There was no indication that anyone ever used the space, let alone tainted it with cooking. The white marble-effect quartz worktops were gleaming. The vast solid walnut and brass dining table must have easily equalled the housekeeper's gross annual salary. In the middle of it sat a generously waisted Fornasetti vase bursting with a magnificent bouquet of blush pink hydrangeas, cream roses and viburnum.

'They're gorgeous, aren't they? Johnny is such an attentive husband.' Margaret had noticed the direction of

Lucia's gaze. Her expression was impenetrable – either she had no control over her facial muscles, or she was a great liar.

'Have you lived here long?' Lucia was keen to divert the conversation to their neighbour.

'Going on six years now. The twins were nine months when we moved in. I remember it like it was yesterday – such a sweet age. Exhausting though, seeing how they were both such early walkers. Oh, you should have seen the house. It was a disaster. Hardest six months of my life, living on a building site with two toddlers, handling the builders, the cleaner, the nanny. Johnny was always out, of course. I think I'm due an honorary degree in business management.' There was absolutely no irony in her pronouncement.

'It's such a good area for families. It helps having friendly neighbours, of course,' Lucia said.

'Oh, it does. Alla was such a darling. She never once complained about the noise, and there's plenty, as you can imagine. I just can't believe she's gone. Did they work out what it was? I hear the police have been back at the Hall.' If she harboured any animosity towards the Professor, it was skilfully concealed.

'I guess they're just going through the motions, seeing how it was a sudden death. I envy you. My downstairs neighbours are frightful. Any tiny noise and they're at my door. You'd think I keep elephants.'

Margaret laughed. 'Oh, how irritating. Some people just exist to make others' lives miserable. We have done well. Alla was never anything but charming. She's very much missed.' The last statement was a polite utterance rather than heartfelt. 'Well, I thought we could wander upstairs. I really like what you did with the Arts and Crafts house you showed me. Now why didn't I think of that? The Apothecary's Garden wallpaper is just the ticket for Lily's room.'

In the space of less than an hour, Margaret's taste had undergone a 360-degree turn. In two years' time, the plain colours would undoubtedly make a comeback as yet another remodelling loomed.

The sleeping quarters bore no aesthetic surprises. There were four bedrooms, with virtually no concessions made to differentiate between the occupants. The children had been allowed a few prints illustrating popular nursery rhymes, a shelf of books and a toy basket each. The master bedroom was as washed out as Lucia had come to expect, apart from something she glimpsed out of the corner of her eye.

'May I use the bathroom?'

'Of course. Just here on the left.'

Lucia opened and closed the indicated door, then tiptoed to her intended destination. On the sofa at the end of the bed were two gift bags in sober black and white with the unmistakable camellia. Judging by their volumes, one contained a handbag and the other perfume. She pressed the flush button and made her way back downstairs.

Margaret was perched on the stool, fidgeting with her phone. 'Another coffee?'

'Thank you, but I'd better get back to Beatrice Hall. I'm very much looking forward to starting here. It's such a pleasure working with like-minded people.'

'Likewise. I think that together we can really transform this place.' Margaret could barely contain her excitement at having been promoted to deputy designer. As for Lucia's part, she hoped Johnny would nix the commission. The most unbearable clients were those that constantly breathed down your neck while you were trying to get the job done, casting themselves as your trusty assistant, only to change hats and shout out irrational orders on a whim.

Lucia got herself a sandwich and sat in her van. She still had a few minutes left before it would start looking like she wasn't taking her work seriously. Just enough time to fill Carliss in. 'On that basis, I'm inclined to think her husband's having an affair.'

'Or he could be a genuinely nice bloke who buys his wife treats,' the detective retorted, sounding like he thought her conclusion was a tad far-fetched this time.

'Seriously? You won't get much change from two hundred pounds for those flowers. And not even hotshot commercial barristers buy their wives Chanel on a whim.'

'Maybe it's her birthday.'

'I think I wouldn't have heard the end of it if it had been. She told me just about everything else that was going on. Oddly laconic about the flowers though. No, nobody buys gifts that extravagant unless it's to assuage guilt.'

'OK, let's imagine you're right. What's that got to do with the Professor?'

'I don't know yet. But I think we might fill in some gaps if we can find out the identity of the mistress.'

'And how exactly are you planning to do that?'

'I thought you didn't want to hear about my methods.'

The few seconds of silence indicated that DCI Carliss had dug himself into a hole. 'Well, I've changed my mind. Full disclosure from now on, so I can keep tabs on you. Snooping around people's houses – you're a bit of a loose cannon, aren't you?'

'How else did you think I could find out what I just told you? In any case, please do join me. Let's leave it till tomorrow though. I need to put in some more hours at Beatrice Hall.'

'Alright, we're on. Famous last words, no doubt. What about the argument between John Walker and the Professor?'

'Nothing from Margaret. She maintains it was all hunky-dory between them.'

'Time for a telephone chat with the man himself, then. Speak to you later, Lucia.'

Chapter 20

DCI Carliss looked at the time and hoped his interviewee wouldn't be in court. The phone didn't ring for long, and the clerk put him through straightaway.

'Hello, John Walker speaking.' A rigid, expertly honed advocate's voice.

'Mr Walker. I'm sorry to bother you at work. It's Detective Chief Inspector David Carliss from the Metropolitan Police. It's about the death of Professor Alla Kiseleva. I wondered if you could spare a few minutes. Just a follow-up from your statement.'

John Walker sounded unimpressed. 'Yes, if you must. I've already imparted everything I know to your colleagues. I'm in the middle of something, so can you please make it quick?'

Carliss wasn't used to being addressed in this manner. The criminal barristers he knew were considerably more gracious – probably because they earned a lot less. 'I'll be very quick. About ten days ago you went to visit the Professor at Beatrice Hall and were heard arguing with her. Can you tell me what that was about?'

The detective got his deserved comeuppance. The line was silent for a second or two, long enough to confirm that John Walker had been caught on the back foot. 'Oh yes, that. Silly thing really. I'd forgotten about it altogether. The fence between our gardens had started leaning over. I went through the title deeds, and it emerged the Professor was responsible for mending it. I paid her a visit to let her know, politely of course, that this was the case. She disagreed. We had a robust discussion, but she relented. She had the fence replaced a few days after, so that was the end of it.'

It was a credible enough explanation, as well as conveniently unverifiable unless Mrs Byrne had been eavesdropping. That was easy to check, but Carliss doubted that a man like John Walker would be so stupid as to produce a lie that could be easily exposed.

'Thank you for clearing that up, Mr Walker. That's all from me. Have a good day.'

The abruptness with which the receiver was replaced at the other end suggested the barrister wasn't accustomed to having to explain himself, especially not to a policeman with ideas above his station.

Carliss looked at his daily to-do list. On the case of Professor Alla Kiseleva, there was only one outstanding task to be completed – an appointment with her solicitor. Morris Llewellyn LLP was nestled at the Strand end of Chancery Lane. Having been bequeathed its substantial offices in the 1890s, it had held its own against the larger marauders responsible for inflating commercial property prices. The more recent glass extension would have undoubtedly offended the Victorian sensibilities of Sir Peregrine Morris, conservative as it may have been compared to its neighbours' bombastic efforts. The Professor's will fell under the jurisdiction of Julius Platt, a descendant of the other co-founder by a tortuous route. The small meeting room was in the newer part of the building, bland but adequately equipped. Julius Platt did not keep the DCI waiting for long. He had just made partner, an achievement which had regrettably coincided with the birth of his first child. He would have been wholly within his rights to take paternity leave, but he didn't judge it wise at a time when the firm was contemplating linking partners' pay to performance. He looked broken.

'Thank you for agreeing to give up your time, Mr Platt. As you know, I'm investigating the death of a client of yours, Professor Alla Kiseleva. When we spoke on the phone, you intimated you have information that you're in a position to voluntarily disclose to the police.'

Julius Platt sat on one of the straight-backed chairs and immediately wished he had campaigned for an increase in the meeting room budget. It was cold and uncomfortable.

'Detective Chief Inspector, I thought it would be best to meet in person. The situation is too irregular and convoluted to explain on the phone.' He took a deep breath and blinked profusely. His pulse was through the roof, and he was horribly light-headed. What he most wanted was to lie down on the abrasive carpeted floor and have a nap. No such luck. 'Before I go into details, I should preface this meeting with the mention that I'm permitted to disclose the information by the written instruction of Professor Kiseleva herself.'

'Why did she give that sort of permission?' Carliss was fully aware of the rules on legally privileged information, especially as nobody was being interviewed as a suspect.

'She was concerned that the actions she was about to take could pose a threat to her life.'

Carliss mentally celebrated what he considered to be the first real breakthrough in the case. 'In what way?'

'She rang me about three weeks ago with the intention to amend her will. There were two beneficiaries under the original will – her nephew Adam Corcoran for Beatrice Hall, and the Collaborative Mathematical Society for the rest of her estate, which comprised funds held in a savings account. The new will was to have a single beneficiary for both the house and the money – the Society.'

Carliss did not expect this particular bombshell. 'So, you're saying she wanted to disinherit Adam?'

'Yes, in no uncertain terms. She also posted instructions for me to release the details of her old and new wills to the authorities, should they require them. I did point out this was not the done thing, but she absolutely insisted. Her precise words were: "I'm afraid this might cost me my life." I assume she referred to the change in the will.'

'Did she say what she was afraid of?'

'No, and I didn't probe. It wasn't my place to.'

'Did she make the new will?'

'I drafted it as per her instructions. There was a bit of a delay – my wife and I have a new baby, you see. I had it ready for her to sign a few days later. Here's the date of the appointment.' It was the first working day after the Professor's death. 'Of course, she never turned up, which means the old will still stands.'

Carliss recalled the other, more crucial question he meant to ask. 'These instructions – were they signed by her?'

'Yes, they were signed, dated and witnessed.'

'Who was the witness?'

Julius Platt consulted the folder he had brought in with him. 'Orla Byrne, of the same address. She put her occupation down as housekeeper.'

Chapter 21

DCI Carliss woke up feeling like his head was in a slowly tightening clamp. He'd been studiously ignoring the tell-tale signs the evening before – a dull ache behind the left eye and a general malaise that he had put down to the broken sleep caused by the puzzling case of Professor Alla Kiseleva. The lurgy was in full swing. The bedside clock unforgivingly read seven eighteen. His appointment with Dr Edmund Glover was scheduled for eight thirty. The protracted telephone negotiations had made it clear that this was a reluctantly granted favour. The rationale behind the early timing was to minimise the interruption to Dr Glover's packed schedule.

The surgery was high up on Heath Street, by the Quaker meeting house. It was private, of course – the Professor would hardly have entrusted herself to the NHS. Despite the corporate glossiness of the glass box waiting room, the subsequently added shopfront couldn't avoid being a scar on the eighteenth-century building. The place was redolent of an upmarket hairdresser's, complete with sleek receptionist, choice magazines and an oversized TV screen. An hour to discuss your real or imaginary ailments with a sympathetic medical professional, unaffected by public sector pressures, cost nearly two hundred pounds. Considering what most wares were being peddled for on Hampstead High Street, this seemed remarkably good value.

'Dr Glover is ready to see you now.'

The office followed in the footsteps of the waiting room, with the addition of a pair of very inviting high-backed armchairs in a corner, where consultations were evidently conducted. Carliss very much doubted they would be used for this particular meeting.

Dr Glover stood up from behind his desk to greet his visitor. His handshake was firm, but not crushing – something he had refined over the years.

'Won't you sit down, Inspector?'

Apart from a notepad, opened at a blank page and accompanied by a discreetly expensive fountain pen, and a latest generation desktop, the white desk was bare. Dr Glover's dress code was traditional smart casual – blazer, shirt, immaculate chinos and brogues. He was the sort of man who kept a tie in the desk drawer for impromptu visits to his club. Everything about him was very precise – his sharp vulpine features, his cropped grey hair, the cut of his clothes, the slim watch on his wrist. He exuded perfect control. Behind his chilly politeness he made no effort to hide the disdain of the soldier towards the inferior policeman. Carliss hoped the painkillers wouldn't wear off. It wasn't going to be pleasant.

'Thank you for seeing me, Dr Glover. I just have a few routine follow-up questions.' Dr Glover glanced at his watch. Carliss had been allocated half an hour, and he wasn't going to be entitled to a single extra minute. 'How long have you known Professor Alla Kiseleva?'

Dr Glover fixed him with a pair of interrogator's eyes. He wasn't used to being on the other side of the table. 'Just under five years, when she became my patient.'

'And you became friends? She invited you to her social occasions.' Despite the apparent banality of the question, the detective felt like he was treading on dangerous ground.

'We were friendly acquaintances. She was a fascinating woman. We enjoyed talking about her work.'

The clipped answers were making it hard to elicit any useful information. Carliss decided to experiment with a shock tactic.

'The post-mortem results indicate the Professor died from poisoning with sodium fluoroacetate. Are you familiar with it?'

Dr Glover slowly cupped his hands together, his rigid fingers not quite grasping their counterparts. His expression was unchanged. 'I know of it. It's a rodenticide. How could she have ingested it?'

'That's something we're still working on. To your knowledge, did she ever exhibit any depressive tendencies?'

'You think it was suicide?'

'We can't rule it out.'

'Evidently, I'm not in a position to disclose her medical records, but no – she wasn't depressed, not insofar as I could tell.'

'Were you aware there was a tin of the poison in her house? In the kitchen, to be precise.'

'No, I had no idea. I've never been in the kitchen at Beatrice Hall.'

'Even though you've known the Professor for five years?'

Dr Glover wasn't one to keel over in cross-examination. A minuscule smile stretched out his thin lips. 'I don't make it my business to snoop around my patients' houses, DCI Carliss.'

The detective wiped his brow. He felt hot and cold at the same time. Dr Glover sensed his weakness and pounced.

'Are you quite alright, Inspector? Would you like some paracetamol?'

'If you don't mind. It's just a pesky cold. Sorry to be a bother.'

'No bother at all.'

Within a few seconds of his picking up the phone, the nurse came in bearing two tablets and a glass of water. Carliss swallowed the lot thirstily.

'Thank you. That'll sort it out.' He tried to refocus his mind on the interview. It was frustratingly blank.

'Was there anything else, Inspector?'

'Yes. Yes, there was one more thing. I've read your account of the party. Did you notice anything out of the ordinary that day, anyone present acting in an unusual manner?'

Dr Glover contemplated the question with the same concentration he would have applied to the wine list at the In and Out.

'Nothing technically out of the ordinary.'

'But there was something that caught your attention?'

'When I arrived at four sharp, Adam Corcoran was on his telephone in the entrance hall. He didn't see me come in. He was having a heated discussion as far as I could tell. He ended it with some rather bad language.' Dr Glover was clearly intending to keep up the suspense – the information was trickling out at a glacial pace.

'What did he say?'

'I quote: "Fucking bitch, she's ruined my life. She's going to pay for it."'

'Do you know whom he was referring to?'

'Absolutely no idea.'

'What happened next?'

'He saw me and cut the conversation short. He muttered a hello and scuttled off to the garden.'

'Did you talk to him during the party?'

'Only cursorily. He seemed embarrassed at my having overheard him.'

'Why didn't you mention this during the first interview?'

'Nobody asked me to report on the whereabouts of the other guests.'

'Are there any other whereabouts that you think are worth mentioning?'

'None, as far as I can recall.'

This was as much as Carliss could take. The medication would soon kick in, but he needed to lie down. The combination of the lurgy and the unexpected role reversal – whereby he had become the vulnerable party – had finished him off.

'Thank you, Dr Glover. That's all for now. If you do remember anything else of note, please give me a ring any time.'

The policeman couldn't remember how he got home. He must have hailed a taxi – there was no way he could have walked or negotiated public transport in that state. Before he fell into the kind of profound sleep that either heralded recovery or a prolonged illness, he managed to text Lucia to postpone the search for John Walker's supposed mistress.

He must have slept for over eighteen hours, uninterrupted. It was four in the morning when he woke up, desperate for a glass of water. He took another dose and went back to bed.

In her flat, Lucia debated what to do. She would leave him to sleep it off and give him a ring on the Monday morning.

When she did, he answered almost straightaway.

'Still alive?'

'Yes, just about. You can't get rid of me that easily.' The weekend-long hibernation, in conjunction with an invalid's diet of buttered toast, bananas and water, had done him good. He still wasn't a hundred percent, but the improvement was considerable.

'How did it go with the good doctor?'

'About as fun as pulling teeth. You're right, he is reptilian. Terrifying too. Ex-army, according to what we've unearthed, so wouldn't have expected any less.' Carliss reported the story about Adam. 'If he was referring to the Professor, the noose is tightening.'

The odds certainly looked well stacked against Adam Corcoran, Lucia thought. 'OK. Now here's the plan on John Walker. He's told Margaret he's working late tonight – I know because I phoned her with the excuse of running some decorating ideas past them both this evening. We go to his chambers and see what he's up to.'

'That sounds like a recipe for disaster. On the other hand, I'm better off coming with you so I can keep you in check.'

'What else are you going to do on your sick day? We're all set then. I'll come pick you up at five.'

Chapter 22

5 Fresenius Court, the chambers of Christian Etherington QC and obscurely named after an eighteenth-century German jurist, sat in the south-eastern corner of Lincoln's Inn. For generations, the first born male Etheringtons had all been given the same name, signalling that, whatever his personal aspirations may be, the heir was inextricably bound to the family business. The present Christian Etherington was acutely aware of the legacy of the founder, his great-grandfather – it had cost him two failed marriages and the same number of crippling financial settlements. The consolation was that his chambers was top of the list every time the big litigators hunted for counsel. John Walker was the name they often asked for – QC quality at junior prices, though it was rumoured the value for money wasn't likely to last much longer. A discerning choice of financial services work had cemented his position as a 'rising star' in the Legal 500 and was meticulously paving his way to silk. Lucia insisted they should go in her van. Carliss was sceptical as to how they would wangle their way in but could see she had a plan. His curiosity got the better of him.

At the main gate, the modern red and white barriers stood ominously closed, in case the knobbly towers and fierce lion rampant on the coat of arms hadn't provided a sufficient hint. The freshly painted van bearing her unadulterated business name waited for the porter to approach.

'I'm working at 5 Fresenius Court. They're expecting me for a last-minute job.'

The man fished out a visitor's pass and waved them through, no questions asked.

'How did you do that?'

'They're having work done to the building. Besides, no one questions tradespeople.'

It was the gateway to a secret London, accessible to all, unknown or of no interest to most. The cloistered community reminded Lucia of her old Cambridge college – authoritative, intimidating and removed from reality, which was the working definition of a barrister. Carliss, who was spared any such associations, was enjoying his procedurally suspect adventure. Star-struck by the daunting majesty of the enclave, he even insisted on a detour via the kitchen garden before she peeled him away. She firmly drew the line at the chapel, and they settled on a bench in the quiet square in direct sight of the door, van at the ready. They could do nothing but wait.

For a good forty-five minutes they watched the inhabitants of 5 Fresenius Court trickle in and out of the building – suits, wigs, gowns, bundles tied with pink tape and wheelie suitcases groaning with court documents. Commercial justice was a lucrative business. They were both drifting off, distracted by the picturesque environment, when John Walker finally made an appearance. His brand-new Porsche 911 Turbo S convertible, which Lucia had been admiring, was parked steps from the door – one of the many perks of the job. He threw his garb on the back seat and revved up the powerful engine. The only criticism was the unadventurous choice of colour – she would have chosen something bolder than white. Still, it fitted with the Walkers' unimaginative home and was a predictable choice for a lawyer.

All this chat was wasted on the detective. He viewed cars as a way of getting from A to B, so the beauty of the present specimen was entirely lost on him. His own vehicle was an offensively gold Corsa that nobody else wanted to touch, optimistically patched up over the years. 'Quick, let's go,' he urged Lucia.

The van started abruptly, and they followed John Walker out of the gate. He weaved effortlessly through the early evening traffic, down and along Fleet Street, heading west. Lucia's minimal use of the brakes ensured they stayed closely behind him. Carliss felt sick and held on tight. He avoided driving wherever he could, and his style was of the sedate variety. The route was part car advert, part involuntary sightseeing tour of London – past Somerset House, Trafalgar Square, St James's Park, Hyde Park Corner and the Royal Albert Hall. The Porsche pulled over outside the Whole Foods on Kensington High Street, hazards on. Walker jumped out and went in. He emerged less than five minutes later clutching a bottle of champagne, only to find the traffic warden had already slapped a yellow ticket on his windscreen. He threw it on the ground and sped off.

'So that's how lawyers treat the Highway Code. I should have known, judging from your maniacal driving,' remarked Carliss.

Lucia wasn't surprised. The council would have been ripped to shreds by Walker's pupil in the traffic tribunal – assuming it ever came to that.

They took a right turn on Phillimore Gardens, where the purring vehicle ground to a halt in front of a semi-detached white stucco house which made its Belsize Park equivalents look like squats. The steps were adorned with two urns bearing ostentatious red azaleas, which were being fastidiously watered by a slight, dark-haired woman. Her short, smooth bob and bright crimson nails, finished off with a Japanese cross-back apron which had just been announced fashionable, indicated she was not domestic staff.

'Well, well, well. He's done alright for himself. Nice lady at home and another one on the go. What do they see in him?' Carliss asked.

'Money, power, the usual.' He wasn't unattractive either. Lucia wondered if Margaret really had no inkling of the affair.

'Mind you, the mistress seems a bit older than the wife, which is not so common.'

Lucia had just spotted this, and an incipient thought began to take shape.

They didn't have to wait long for an indication of the nature of the relationship between John Walker and his host. There was no obvious kiss, only a tender arm around her waist as they went in. That they were intimate was unmistakable.

'There you go. Now we find out who she is.' Lucia whipped out her phone.

'How? I could phone the station and ask someone to look into her.'

Lucia laughed at his technological ineptitude. 'You don't need to call the station. Land Registry records are publicly available. For a few pounds, we'll know exactly what she's called.' She typed in the address and waited patiently for the title register to download.

'She could be renting.' Carliss was evidently a little embarrassed at his own lack of initiative.

'Nobody rents a house like that. Besides, have you seen her? She hardly looks like the renting type. Here it is. One owner – Frieda Marie Alexander. You won't believe how much this place cost. Now let's see what she's been up to.' Lucia typed in her name. Her supposition was instantly confirmed.

'What is it?'

'I suspected as much.'

They pored over the screen, eyes widening as they read on.

Mrs Justice Alexander belonged to a rare and readily identifiable breed. She was one of the few women judges to sit in the Commercial Court, where John Walker primarily plied his trade. Lucia read out the entry: 'Born in Tokyo to a British diplomat and a Japanese hotel heiress. One of the youngest women to take silk.' In the official photo, her delicate face and billowing, expertly tailored dress ensured she stood out in a sea of greying men.

'You know what you said about money and power? Seems like you got it the wrong way round at the outset.'

Lucia admitted she had. 'I should have known better. He was unlikely to swap his own housewife for another.'

The newly revealed information was dynamite. Lucia made a mental note to check how many cases Frieda Alexander had sat on that John Walker had won. Either way, career suicide loomed for both parties. How intelligent people could be so utterly stupid was beyond her – but then, in their boundless arrogance, they must have assumed they were invincible – a major defect that came with the professional territory.

'He's in a lot of trouble, that's for sure. Titillating as this may be, what's it got to do with our murder?' said Carliss.

Lucia could tell the inspector was having more fun than he was willing to admit. 'Nothing, perhaps. For now, at least, it's just a useful fact to bank. You look like you could do with some rest. I'll take you home.'

For once, it was Carliss who was being looked after, which was unprecedented. Given the pain had started again on the left side of his head, he was grateful. Lucia promised to drive more smoothly, and before long they were on the edges of Regent's Park, back to the familiarity of North London. Carliss had dozed off. She touched his arm gently to wake him up. 'You're still unwell. Don't do any more work. And that's an order.'

'OK, boss. So far, we've got a grieving housekeeper, a so-called nephew cut out of the inheritance, a shifty PA, an inscrutable doctor and a cheating husband. Oh, and a long-suffering wife who may or may not know what working after hours really means. Who's the killer?'

'Go to bed. Tomorrow's another day.'

She watched him go in and close the door behind him. Now that he'd been safely delivered, she needed some time to think. Her head was spinning with the attributes of their six suspects, but nothing fell into place. She would have to sleep on it, and in the meantime, she would drop off the van at home and head to the Red Lion. There was no trouble in the world that a large glass of chilled Burgundy couldn't alleviate.

* * *

The boozer was respectably populated for a Monday night. Come to think of it, Lucia had never seen it empty. Bills, children, partners and overbearing parents could all be momentarily eradicated by a few cold pints. She approached the bar and sat next to a young lad she hadn't seen there before. He was well bedded on the stool and fixed her with an uncensored suggestive expression.

'Alright, love? Here on your own?'

'Save your breath, I'm not on the pull. Hi, Becky.' She indicated her usual with a raised finger and gave the unsuspecting lad a condescending look.

Becky, resplendent in a low-cut top, watched the exchange with an expectant look, hoping for entertainment.

'Oh, don't be like that. Give us a smile.' He persevered, despite the unequivocal response to his advances. There was something off about him that intoxication alone didn't explain. He stared at her with enlarged pupils surrounded by reddened whites. His breathing was visibly shallow, and his fingers shook on the beer glass.

Lucia brushed it off. His health wasn't her business. 'Pack it in, or I'll give you a slap, and you're never coming back here again.'

He grinned in vain for a moment longer and turned away, despondent at his failed romantic overture. She savoured the first sip of the buttery wine and blinked. She couldn't stop turning over in her head what Carliss had uncovered at Morris Llewellyn. Nearly all the pieces pointing at Adam as the main suspect were in place. What she couldn't quite reconcile was the role that Mrs Byrne played in the whole charade. One to squeeze out of her, if she was at all amenable to another session in the makeshift confessional. Mrs Byrne was perfectly capable of holding back information so long as nobody asked any direct questions.

The noisy chatter around her was grating. They seemed particularly elated about something.

'What's up with them?'

Becky shook her head. 'Beats me. I think the football must have been on earlier. They're all mad for it, this lot.'

'Don't let anyone take my seat.'

'Got it. Don't hold it against Kev, by the way. He's new and hasn't learned the ropes yet. He tried it with me the other day, but he just doesn't give up. Not many girls around here to practise on.' Becky laughed forgivingly.

Lucia stood up and slunk past the red-faced men shouting and swilling their glasses, spilling beer on the already objectionable carpet. They all had bloodshot eyes. The men's and women's toilets faced each other. As she came out, she nearly walked into Jimbo, Danny's apprentice. The door hovered open for a few seconds before he let it slam behind him. It was long enough for Lucia to see Adam. The tightly rolled-up banknote was the ideal conduit for the thin line of white powder to make the journey from the countertop into his system. He was too engrossed in this activity to notice he had an audience. Jimbo's eyes were glazed over. He didn't recognize her, and, even if he had, the encounter would have been forgotten by the morning.

Chapter 23

The invitation sat on the kitchen table, a pithy text handwritten in spidery looped cursive on a thick, orange-bordered card – "Walter and Nina, At Home, Thursday 1st October at 7pm". It came in the morning post. Nina had never been one for advance planning, not that Lucia had any other plans. She had meant to arrange a catch-up with her old friend ever since Carliss's Home Office connections had failed to shed any light on the Professor. The party was something to look forward to in the midst of all the unhappiness. Lucia briefly entertained the idea of the inspector as a plus one but decided against it. She had important business that could only be discussed in private. If her plan worked, she could come clean to Carliss in due time.

Lucia reprimanded herself at the distraction. Now was not the time to indulge in thoughts about how an evening in Belgravia might be spent. The chance sighting of Adam in a very compromising position at the Red Lion had given her fresh ammunition. She drained the rest of her coffee cup and got up to go. She had taken a leaf out of Frieda Alexander's book and bought herself a cross-back apron on the way back from Holland Park. It made a welcome change from the overalls. She wore it with a pair of nurse's slacks from the army surplus shop – a pleasingly pioneer woman ensemble.

At Beatrice Hall, Lucia was taken aback to find Mrs Byrne polishing the doorknobs. It smacked of displacement activity, given the state of the rest of the house.

'Mrs Byrne, I need to talk to you.' Lucia put on her best fraught face. She had turned over in her mind what approach to take. It was unlikely the housekeeper would make a voluntary disclosure this time, so whatever knowledge she was holding on to would have to be somehow prized out of her.

'Yes, of course.' There was noticeable panic in her voice. 'Are you OK, child? You don't look too well.'

'Let's go down to the kitchen if you don't mind. I don't want us to be overheard.'

They descended the stairs into the kitchen. Mrs Byrne sat down, and Lucia could almost smell her fear, as if she were waiting for the skies to open up.

'I don't know if I should be telling you this.' Lucia frowned and fidgeted with the hem of her apron. The outfit gave her an air of efficient innocence that was well suited to the occasion.

Mrs Byrne's eyes widened. 'What is it?'

Tears welled up and were suppressed.

'Just get it off your chest, love. I'm here to listen.' The tension in the room had palpably decreased, as intended, so as to maximize the shock value of what was about to come.

'It's Adam. The police think he's killed the Professor.'

If there ever was any blood in Mrs Byrne's face, it was gone now. She looked like she couldn't make her mind up whether to faint or vomit. She sat motionless, like an animal hunted out of its hiding place that knew it stood no chance.

'They found out about the new will. That makes him the main suspect.'

This fresh blow broke the housekeeper. She started panting heavily and held her head with violently shaking hands. Lucia thought she might be foaming at the mouth but couldn't be sure. She waited. After a few minutes that felt as long as hours, the panic attack started to subside. Mrs Byrne stood up to fetch herself a glass of water, which she downed with white-knuckled fingers.

'How do you know all this?' The question brimmed with fear and suspicion.

'I overheard that inspector on the phone – you know, when he was hanging around the other day. He said they're planning to take him in for questioning. I don't understand. What's the new will? And what's that got to do with Adam?' The room had suddenly become very hot, and Lucia realised she was genuinely anxious as to whether the gamble would pay off.

The housekeeper stared at the sink, which was as neglected as it had always been. Her breathing had steadied, and she had an air of downtrodden resignation about her.

'The Professor was going to cut him out of the will. He was supposed to inherit the house. She wanted to leave everything to that godforsaken institution of hers.'

'But if she changed her will, that puts him in the clear. There'd be no point killing her if he was already disinherited.' Lucia surmised what the retort would be and hoped that Mrs Byrne would continue to play ball.

'She hadn't changed it before she died.'

'How do you know?'

'I witnessed a letter to her solicitor. And I overheard her on the phone. She was going to see him on the 7th, the Monday after… after the party, to sign the new will.' Her voice faltered.

'And Adam knew this?'

'I told him everything.'

'Was that why you were arguing in the kitchen?'

'Yes. Yes, it was.' Mrs Byrne gave out a low moan. 'Oh, what have I done? I've lied to the police.'

'What do you mean?'

'I told them we were arguing about Adam's drinking.' A realisation had just dawned, and the housekeeper's eyes narrowed menacingly. The fear had given way to defensiveness which, coupled with desperation, could jeopardize the whole exercise. 'Did you tell them about that?'

'I had to. They really ground me down with their relentless questioning. They made me feel like I was guilty, though I haven't done anything.' Lucia's bottom lip quivered, and she suppressed another tear.

Mrs Byrne's cornered look mollified a little. The shared experience of police intimidation was something that could alleviate Lucia's perceived betrayal. 'Oh, they had no mercy with me either. Talked to me like I was a common criminal. I told them everything I knew, except for the reason behind the row. No good would have come from telling the truth. It would only have made Adam look bad.' She leaned forward, and Lucia caught a glimpse of the mother grieving for her lost child. 'He couldn't have hurt the Professor. They might not have seen eye to eye of late, but he hasn't got it in him. I know him like I knew my own…' She stopped abruptly. She couldn't face bringing up that painful subject again.

'Why were you arguing, Mrs Byrne?'

'He asked me to keep an eye on her. She'd been behaving oddly – cold and dismissive – and he didn't know what he'd done wrong. Perhaps she'd had enough of him living here, and his drinking…' She couldn't help veering back to the delicate subject. 'When he told her he'd lost his job, she was livid. Said she didn't want a layabout moping around the house, leeching off her. Leeching – as if! She barely paid him, for all the running around he did for her. When I told him about the change in the will, he was beside himself. All that time being her slave, and this is how she repays him. Oh, it makes me sick.' She was properly incensed now, and Lucia calculated she could probe a little further.

'I can't believe the Professor didn't leave you anything. All those years of loyal service. It's an affront.'

Lucia had barely finished talking when the housekeeper opened her mouth to speak, then thought better of it. The cogs were turning feverishly.

'Mrs Byrne, the police will find you out sooner or later. They know you witnessed the Professor's letter to the solicitor. If you don't tell the truth, they'll have you down as a suspect as well. They'll say you and Adam connived to get rid of her for the inheritance. I've seen what they're like – they want to pin this on someone so they can close the case.' Lucia's plea was the last weapon in her arsenal. If that didn't work, nothing else would.

Mrs Byrne sat motionless, hands crossed on the table, biting the inside of her cheek for comfort. When she finally spoke, it was as if she'd been hypnotized. 'He said he'd give me some of the money from selling the house if I kept an eye on her. She didn't leave me a penny, and I gave my best years to this place. I didn't do anything wrong. I didn't kill her. I hated her, but I couldn't take a life.'

Lucia had what she wanted. Trying to squeeze any more out of the woman would have been fruitless.

'I just want all of this to end.' It was Mrs Byrne who was crying this time, and the tears were very real.

'I know. They'll catch whoever did this, and it'll end.' The experience had been intense, and even Lucia was worn out. 'You don't mind if I go home, Mrs Byrne? I'm done in. I've not slept because of this madness.'

'No, you go home. They've put us all through the wringer, and for what?' She rose slowly. 'I'd better finish upstairs. Don't know why I'm bothering, really. Adam's barely ever here these days.'

Lucia held back from imparting the probable explanation for his absence. It wouldn't have achieved anything. She suspected the housekeeper didn't know about his cocaine habit.

Chapter 24

It wasn't even midday when Lucia got in. She didn't normally drink that early, but she felt the circumstances justified it. She poured herself the dregs of the bottle in the fridge door and sat staring out of the window. A woman was pushing a buggy with a dog nearing its expiry date. Joggers in lustrous attire strode purposefully into the coffee shop. There were two suspects with decent motives, and she knew Carliss would be tempted to make an arrest. The doorbell interrupted her concentration. She wasn't expecting anyone.

'Afternoon. You're not busy, are you?' The detective had walked up and stood expectantly in the corridor, water dripping off his mac. A puddle was starting to form, so Lucia had no choice but to invite him in.

'Come in.'

He clocked the half empty glass of wine on the counter. 'A bit early, isn't it?'

'It's been a long morning. What is it you want to talk about?' She wasn't in the mood for company. The thinking that needed to be done in preparation for Nina's party required solitude.

None of this registered with Carliss. He was obliviously bright-eyed in the way that only a recovered invalid could be. 'I thought we could go through what we've got to date. It looks like we're very close to cracking it.' She could tell he was looking forward to shelving the whole unfortunate affair – petty crime, or whatever it was that he busied himself with when he wasn't chasing a murderer, must have never seemed so appealing in comparison.

'Tea?'

'Sure, if you're making it.' He sank into one of the armchairs at the living room end of the open-plan kitchen. 'It's nice, this place. Light.'

Lucia returned a knowing smile. On the rare occasions that she had visitors to her flat, they always had to rack their brains for a more substantial compliment. The best anyone could come up with was 'minimalist'. The place was empty and soulless. It didn't match the artistic output at Beatrice Hall. As she handed Carliss the drink, his eyes drifted to the wall of books.

'Nice bookcase.' He grasped his tea and stood up to take a closer look. 'Wallace Stegner. One of my favourite writers. Have you read *Angle of Repose*?'

Her tired eyes lit up a touch. 'Too navel-gazing for my taste.'

'I wouldn't have had you pegged as a fan of *Crossing to Safety*,' he said.

'"We made plenty of mistakes, but we never tripped anybody to gain an advantage, or took illegal shortcuts when no judge was around. We have all jogged and panted it out the whole way." Isn't that something to live by?' She was running out of steam, and for once felt like she was the one on edge.

'Sure.' He smiled, surprised at the revelation. 'I didn't realize you're an idealist.'

'We all have our flaws.'

Carliss circled the room and settled at the kitchen table. 'Where are we? Adam's a penniless cokehead. He gets the housekeeper to spy on the Professor in return for a share of the house sale money. It turns out the old girl's planning to cut him out of the inheritance. He hasn't got much time, so he kills her before she can sign the new will. With or without the housekeeper's help – I can't quite figure that one out. I'm minded to bring him in for a proper interview.'

'Aren't you jumping the gun? You've got no proof he poisoned the glass.'

'You'd be surprised what a little judiciously applied pressure can yield.'

Lucia had no appetite for imagining what judiciously applied pressure could yield. 'I just don't think it's as straightforward as it looks. What about everyone else? Are you discounting them without any further thought?'

'No, but we can't ignore the obvious. Adam Corcoran stood to gain substantially from the victim's death, so we've got motive. Dr Glover overheard him threatening the Professor. He may have had an accomplice in Mrs Byrne. The murder wasn't spontaneous – he planned it to stop the new will being executed. The means pinned suspicion on any of the people at the party but made it impossible to focus on a particular individual. If you're right about how the poison was administered, once it was in the coupe all Adam had to do was let it run its course.' He looked very pleased with himself. 'It all adds up, don't you think?'

Lucia wasn't thinking straight anymore, but she certainly wasn't buying it. 'As things stand, we've still got a lot of blanks on Glover, Emilia, and the Walkers.'

'But they may be blanks because there's nothing to fill in,' the inspector argued. 'Anyway, I'm not drawing a line under it just yet. You've got to bear in mind that sometimes the truth just stares you in the face. I'll see you around then.'

Lucia was seething. She picked up the now empty wine glass and decided against opening a fresh bottle. They desperately needed some sort of miracle, a breakthrough.

Chapter 25

It was barely light outside when Lucia woke up on the day of Nina's party. She needed some time away from Beatrice Hall, so she had called in sick. Adam's response had been one of indifference – he clearly had other more pressing concerns. Margaret Walker had left numerous messages begging her to meet, which so far she had ignored. Perhaps it was time to take up the job, if only for a bit of variety. She was due at their house that morning.

In Belsize Park, Margaret Walker opened the door dressed in another ludicrous outfit – a baggy dress, achingly on trend. Lucia was not in a good mood.

'Lucia, hello. Come in.'

'Hi, Margaret. I'm sorry I didn't return your calls. This business with the Professor has been eating up all of my time. Endless questions from the police – and they haven't made an ounce of progress, as far as I can tell.' She reasoned that venting her anger might make her feel better. It wasn't working.

'Oh, I know. Absolutely useless. You'd think that with all the resources our taxes pay for, they could do a better job. Don't even get Johnny started on the public sector.'

They went through to the kitchen, where Margaret busied herself with the daunting coffee machine. Lucia stood by the French windows – beyond their garden lay Beatrice Hall.

And, just like that, something clicked.

'Margaret, is that fence new?'

Margaret had won the battle and was proudly holding two full cups. 'What fence?'

'The one between your garden and the Professor's.'

'That old thing? No, it's been there ever since we moved in.'

'Did you ever have any trouble with it? Was it leaning over at any point?'

'No, it's always been fairly solid. It's funny, I was just saying to Johnny the other day how lucky we are. My friend from barre class has had no end of trouble with her neighbours. Boundary issues cost a lot of money to fix around here.' Margaret was bemused. 'Why do you ask?'

'Oh, just because my fence looks similar, and it's nowhere near as sturdy. The developer must have put in the cheapest kind,' Lucia lied. She didn't even have a garden.

'Awful. Are you in one of these new builds next to the Heath? I've heard terrible things from the other mums at school. Work so shoddy it should be illegal.' Margaret launched into a tirade about how standards had plummeted since EU enlargement, a view very much in keeping with her stance on the public sector. Lucia nodded sympathetically, not taking any of it in. She needed to let Carliss know.

For the following half hour, Margaret did most of the talking. Lucia showed her various mood boards, hoping that information overload would prevent her new client from reaching a decision on the spot. She realized she didn't want to start the job any time soon. It would distract her from the murder. As it happened, Margaret was not the decisive type. Half, if not more of the fun lay in equivocating about endless possibilities. The visit ended as it had begun – Lucia was none the wiser as to the substance of her brief, which suited her just fine. Back in the van, she messaged DCI Carliss: "John Walker lied about the fence. It's not new."

By the time she got home, she was looking forward to the evening ahead. What was she going to wear to the party? She had never been one for hoarding clothes. The end of her old job was a chance to prune down her wardrobe to a few choice pieces, with the rest relegated to the charity shop bin. She pulled out a black velvet kimono with a silk waist tie. It was short and would have looked vulgar with heels – not that she owned any – so she paired it with suede ballet flats in the same colour. She would have a long, indulgent bath before getting ready, which was a luxury she seldom afforded herself. She simply didn't have the patience.

When she emerged, it was five fifty-nine – plenty of time left before she had to be on the move. She dressed herself carefully, stood back and admired her handiwork. The light freckles on her nose attenuated the effect of the stridently red lipstick. The get-up had the desired effect – alluring but not ostentatious. Just as she was applying the finishing touches to her face, the doorbell squealed insistently.

'It's me. I need to talk to you.'

She heard Carliss's hurried steps coming up the stairs as soon as she had pressed the buzzer. She opened the door and beckoned him in.

'Going anywhere?'

Lucia didn't mind his openly admirative stare. If anything, she enjoyed it. 'A party. Do you want a drink?'

'I'll be OK, thanks. Don't want to keep you.'

'What have you got?' She knew it must have been something momentous to warrant a visit – her heart was pounding.

'I spoke to Walker. You're right, he'd been telling porkies all along,' the policeman said excitedly as he sat down at her kitchen table.

'Really?' She was surprised that John Walker had yielded so easily.

DCI Carliss had clearly read her mind. 'He didn't give in from the start. I told him about the fence and asked him what the row with the Professor was really about. He beat around the bush for a while – said he couldn't remember, it wasn't important, the usual rubbish. When I pointed out I knew about Mrs Justice Alexander and suggested a trip to the station for lying to the police, he relented. I don't think he wants to attract attention to himself, given what he came out with next.' He paused for effect.

'Come on, stop trying to be clever,' Lucia joked impatiently.

'Sorry. The Professor knew about the affair and was blackmailing him. Had been for months. That's why they were arguing.'

Even Lucia hadn't seen this one coming. 'Oh, that is good. So, he had plenty of motive to get rid of her.'

'Oh, yes, plenty, given how much there was at stake. His career, his marriage. He had already made a substantial down payment for her silence, but she wanted more. He was worried the wife would get suspicious, so he confronted the Professor. She laughed and said she had him exactly where she wanted him.'

'I imagine someone like John Walker wouldn't take that very well. How did the Professor find out?'

'He didn't know. Assumed she must have spotted them together somewhere in town. He said they were discreet, but we saw them, so she could have done as well.'

'Don't forget we did follow them – not that I'm giving him any credit,' Lucia remarked.

They both smiled.

'You look great, by the way,' the policeman said.

They walked downstairs together, and Lucia got into her taxi to Lygon Place.

Chapter 26

At the other end of town, the glass-fronted door to a magnificent Queen Anne style town house dutifully opened before her. The enormous sisal doormat proudly read "Chanler" in heavy black capitals, lest the guests should forget whose party they had been invited to. It was only ten minutes past seven, but the place was already buzzing. It smelled of fig cologne, and there was silk and soft leather as far as the eye could see. Nina wove her way towards her friend through the crowd – a modern Athena, unapologetic in a burnt-orange sequinned gown that glistened like chainmail.

'Lucia, darling.' Nina drawled her name with an exaggerated Italian accent. '*Bellissima, come sempre.*'

'Nina. It's been too long.'

The women embraced warmly. Lucia had missed her closest friend. They came from such different backgrounds and lived such different lives, and yet every time they met, they could effortlessly pick up where they left off.

'I like what you've done with the place.' It was brash and derivative, and it was Nina all over. The floor to ceiling mirrors cladding a whole drawing room wall reflected the glossy walnut furniture. A young woman, resplendent in red satin under the dimmed chandeliers, leaned against the midnight blue and gold chevron wallpaper. 'You couldn't make it up.'

'Ah, this. I'm getting bored with it. Say, wouldn't you like the job? That way I can have you all to myself.'

'I couldn't improve on it. Don't rip it out.'

Nina shook her mass of blonde curls. She had different colour eyes – one green and one hazel – which could instantly flip from enticing to unsettling. 'You're right, it's not too bad. You should see my new drinks cabinet. I had it shipped all the way from Charleston. They don't make them like that in Europe.' She gestured to the nearest waiter, who dutifully pirouetted in their direction.

'Cheers. I'm so glad you came, Lulu. It's like old times.'

Lucia and Nina Chanler, née Lexington, had been inseparable since university in Cambridge. They had ended up working for the same law firm and even shared an office in their previous life – not that the latter had set foot in one since marrying Walter 'Charming' Chanler, with his South Carolina tinned fish money that had made life in Lygon Place possible. He had wooed his way into what he thought was British high society, or at least the kind of society that Nina frequented. What went on behind closed doors in Belgravia would have shocked the bourgeois sensibilities of North London, which is why Carliss was best left safely parked at home.

'How is your mother?'

Nina cackled. 'On fine form, as always. She's bored rigid with her retirement – she says it's about as fun as waterboarding. Coming from her, that's quite an indictment.'

'Is she here tonight?'

'No, she's gone back north. Oh, I should have known.' Nina affected a playfully wounded look. 'You're just here to use me. You'll have to entertain me with some sparkling conversation before you ask for a favour.'

'The serious business can wait, Double N. I'm here to have a good time.' "Northern Nina", they used to call her at boarding school, and it stuck in a modified form. By tradition, the Lexington children were educated locally until they were old enough to be sent away to the Cheltenham Colleges, where the involuntarily acquired Nottinghamshire accent was swiftly stamped out.

'Miss Lucia. Lovely as ever.' Walter was so parodically Southern as to merit an entire doctoral thesis. He and Nina were a good match. If they hadn't met, she would have ended up marrying and bossing around a questionable diplomat from her mother's circle. To his credit, Walter took his wife with a generous pinch of salt. More importantly, he had impressed Virginia Lexington. 'How's work?'

'Good. Busy. Keeps me out of trouble.'

Walter turned to a rotund woman in head-to-toe emerald green, like a giant Fabergé egg, who hovered expectantly on the fringes of their group. 'Lucia here is the best in the business.' He was always happy to fly the flag for a friend. The Chanlers had always looked out for one another and their close ones, not out of grudging duty or in the expectation that the favour would be returned, but simply because good manners and social responsibility were in their blood. 'In fact, everything you see around you is her doing.' He winked discreetly in Lucia's direction, and Nina grinned. There was no harm in a little promotional exercise.

The ovoid lady beamed. 'Oh, Walter, this place is splendid. You're very talented, Lucia. You could be just the ticket for Oxfordshire.' Predictably, Walter was a guaranteed hit with females of a certain age. 'How do you know the Chanlers?'

'Nina and I used to work together, a long time ago.'

'Oh, you're a lawyer too? How very clever. Do you miss it?'

'Not much. I like the quiet life.'

Walter laughed heartily. 'I don't believe that for a second. You two weren't cut out for the quiet life. You're up to something, Lulu, I can smell it.' His eyes suddenly narrowed as they darted to the door. 'Why, if it isn't Marcus Calthorpe. Nina, he's been dying to meet you.'

'Come along then, Lucia. Let's get introduced.' Nina wound her arm around her friend's waist and strode towards a serious-looking man in an unnecessarily sober suit. 'The new Ambassador to Oman,' she whispered in Lucia's ear. 'Mummy's successor and professional golden boy. Apparently our contemporary at Emmanuel. Never set eyes on him, have you? Must have been one of the studious ones.'

'You mean he was out during daylight hours. No danger of our collective paths ever crossing, in that case.'

Walter did the honours. Marcus Calthorpe looked petrified.

'A pleasure to meet you at last, Marcus.' Nina's disconcerting eyes did little by way of reassurance. 'You're quite the mythical creature. I hear you're going to single-handedly broker peace in the Middle East.'

The poor man flushed all the way to an unpleasant shade of beetroot. 'That's very kind. I'm afraid I've got some rather big shoes to fill.'

Nina laughed charitably. 'Yes, Mother does have big feet. I'm sure you'll do very well. I do hope you enjoy our little get-together.' She flashed her most benevolent smile and disappeared back into the crowd, followed by her old friend. 'I think I've paraded you around enough.' Nina signalled to Lucia. 'Let's have another drink and you can ask me that favour you wanted.'

They settled in a couple of low cocktail chairs safely tucked behind the specially hired martini bar, which was barely keeping up with demand.

'Professor Alla Kiseleva and Dr Edmund Glover. Do those names mean anything to you?'

Nina frowned thoughtfully. 'No… Do you want me to ask Mater?'

'If you could.'

'Dare I ask what it's about?' Nina's eyes were glowing. She knew Lucia was up to no good.

'A murder. Do you want to help me?'

'Oh, I'd kill for it. In a manner of speaking… I'm bored witless buying furniture and going to Walter's work dos. There are only so many conversations on sardine prices that I can grin through.'

The old friends talked and drank for hours and made up for all the time they had been apart. The evening disappeared in a haze of champagne and euphoria. By the end, they lay on the sofa, shoes abandoned on the floor. Walter had retired to bed. It was four in the morning, and they were slowly running out of steam.

'We need a downer, Lulu. I'm too excited to sleep.' Nina stood up and walked upstairs. A few minutes later, she reappeared with a small envelope.

'Sleeping pills? They don't do much for me.'

'Of course they don't. This is much better.'

Lucia opened the envelope. Inside was a sachet of white powder.

'Don't take too much – you're not a horse. K always does the trick – it'll take the edge right off, I promise,' said Nina.

Before abandoning all caution, Lucia checked her phone. The screen glowed with news of a voice message. She listened to Carliss's voice: 'Just a quick one. Harding pulled Danny over for a traffic check. Nothing noteworthy in the van, just a box of donuts and some bananas for the boys. Not giving up yet. Hope you're having a good time.'

Chapter 27

DCI Carliss stood outside the gates at Lygon Place, wondering if he should ring the bell or wait for Lucia. The building made it perfectly clear that entry was subject to a stringent selection process, and he wasn't at all confident he would be successful. Lucia's message had been oddly cryptic – an instruction to be there at nine sharp, to meet a friend of hers that could help. A heavy glass-panelled door swung open, releasing a Filipino nanny and her small charge, bundled out of sight in a comically oversized pram that emulated an age best left behind.

'Are you ready?' Lucia had crept up unnoticed. She had enjoyed watching him, for once out of his element.

'Your friend has done well for herself.' He was lost for words, not knowing what to expect.

'Little Nina always falls on her feet. It's genetic.' Lucia pressed the bell firmly, and the gate clicked open. Nina stood waiting in the doorway, thrilled at the prospect of an adventure.

'Come in, you two. You must be the mysterious inspector. You didn't tell me he was this good-looking, Lulu. Well done.' She weighed him up, as if she were deciding on a purchase in Harrods and shook his hand more vigorously than he had expected. 'Nina Chanler.' She was wearing a marginally less terrifying outfit than at the party – plain jeans and a ruffled shirt last seen on an Elizabethan pirate. The heterochrome eyes and manic corkscrew curls did little to put the newcomer at ease.

In broad daylight and emptied of the guests, the house looked less demi-monde lair and more estate agent's catalogue, though the tastes it catered to were admittedly niche. It was spotlessly clean, no doubt thanks to the efforts of a small army of help. As soon as they sat down in the drawing room, a plainly attired but unmistakably uniformed butler appeared, seemingly out of nowhere, enquiring as to whether they would be taking tea.

'Did Lucia tell you anything, Inspector?' Nina evidently had news to share; she could barely contain herself. Nonetheless, she couldn't resist prolonging the agony a little.

'Not a thing.' Carliss tried to focus on one eye at a time but the wallpaper was giving him a headache.

'Typical Lulu. So secretive.' She laughed at her friend, who grinned back. They knew full well they were playing up the melodrama. 'We used to work together a while back. When she came by on Thursday, she asked me to look into something. I'm… how shall I put it? Best placed to uncover things about people who don't want to be found out.' Nina leaned back, one arm stretched over the velvet sofa. 'But don't for a second imagine I'm going to give it to you on a plate. I want in first.'

Carliss had no idea what she was talking about. 'What do you mean, you want in?'

'I want to be part of the investigation. Lucia has already filled me in on the background. I'm in a position to offer help that you're unlikely to access elsewhere.'

'Great. Another meddling civilian. I'm a bit desperate, so OK, you're in. What have you got for me?' replied the policeman, defeated.

Nina flicked her hair triumphantly. 'Your man Glover was in Eastern Europe in the 1980s. I don't yet know what he was up to or where he was posted, but I've been promised more information.'

'How do you know? More to the point, who are you? I don't like this at all. I know better than to meddle in areas closed off to the ordinary police.'

'Don't worry, I'm not mad, if that's what you're afraid of. I'm lucky enough to have a direct line to the Foreign Office. My mother was an ambassador, and she's banked quite a few favours that she hasn't called in yet. If you don't believe me, you can look her up. Virginia Lexington.'

'And the Professor? Don't tell me she was a Russian spy. This isn't a third-rate film,' replied Carliss in disbelief.

Nina was offended. 'It's not a game, you know. These people do exist. And yes, since you ask. You should thank Lucia for having a good forage through that book the Professor had in the pipeline, otherwise I would have never known where to start. Her file is inaccessible, bar an unmarked photo. It's almost certainly her, though we're talking nearly forty years ago. No name, no personal details, nothing. She must have been pretty special.'

Carliss was out of his depth, and he knew it. 'You know I can't verify any of this. And what's it got to do with her death?'

'We know she can't be Russian,' interrupted Lucia. 'Remember the badly written papers? And, if she was on MI6's radar, they must have known she came to the UK. That leaves two possibilities. Either she was harmless, or she had something valuable to sell.'

'Which one do you think it was?' retorted Carliss.

'She wasn't harmless. I'd venture to guess she was on the run from her own people.'

'Did Glover and the Professor know each other? Back in the day, I mean. To be honest, I'm struggling to see how these titbits, juicy as they sound, relate to our case,' asked the inspector.

'There's nothing to suggest they did,' answered Nina, hopeful that no finality was implied.

'OK, so we've got nothing. Glover was a soldier and a spy – no surprise there. The Professor was Russian, or maybe not Russian, and also a spy, for the other side – also not entirely unexpected. Years later, she gets herself killed by her nephew, who is by far the most likely suspect. I think we've got ourselves side-tracked. It's an open and shut case. I'm not getting myself dragged into this murky web,' protested Carliss.

Nina was angrily chewing on a bright orange nail. 'You mis-sold him, Lulu. He's just another PC Plod. What a waste of time that was.'

'Wait a minute.' Lucia knew she had to rescue the situation. 'Nobody in their right mind believes in coincidences. Until we find out what they were really up to, we can't discount what Nina's found out.'

'We'll need more on Glover if we're to link him to the Professor,' the policeman conceded reluctantly.

The women exchanged satisfied looks.

'That's all we ask for – patience. We've got plenty of gaping holes left.' Nina stretched out like a cat and fixed him with one flickering hazel eye.

Carliss was fidgeting with his hands, pretending to concentrate on his teacup – translucently white with delicate green chinoiserie. Nina could see that their self-assurance made him doubt his own abilities.

'So, you two worked together?' he asked.

Nina took the lead. 'We made a good dastardly duo. All water under the bridge now.' She looked out of the tall window. The sun had given way to relentless rain, and the pavement looked distinctly uninviting. 'Since we understand each other, and with the weather being so filthy, I think we can move on from tea.' A few taps on her phone, and seconds later the obliging butler materialised with the order. Nina waved him out and poured the champagne. She lit a thin cigarette, cross-legged on a soft ottoman.

'You look like a smoking man, Inspector. Can I tempt you?'

He picked one out from the outstretched packet. 'Sobranie. Very nice. A step up from my usual fare.'

'Don't tell me you've given up, Lulu.'

'Not today. Reminds me of the good times. Cheers, Double N.'

The inspector sank back in the armchair, champagne in hand. Lucia reckoned that, given time, he could get used to Belgravia.

Chapter 28

The rain had eased, and Lucia and Carliss were walking side by side through St James's Park, a pleasant detour under the guise of catching the 24 bus back north. The line-up of government buildings on Horse Guards Road served as a stark reminder that the case might easily slip from their grasp. Lucia was acutely aware of what lay on the other side of the river and hoped that the death of the Professor wouldn't end up swallowed in the cavernous belly of Ceauşescu Towers.

'What are you thinking?' she asked.

'I'm thinking this is out of our league.'

'That's why I got Nina involved. She's like a dog with a bone – won't give up till she gets results. Listen, something's bothering me. Have you heard any more from your PC about Danny?'

'As a matter of fact, I haven't. With all these cheap thrills, I forgot all about it. I'll give him a ring right now.' He was about to make the call. 'Hold on, he's already sent me a message. Looks like your Danny's been leaving work every day at four sharp and going to the builders' merchant. Does that answer your question?'

'Sort of. Don't you think that's odd? No builder goes shopping every day.'

'Maybe he's not very organized?'

'Maybe. What did you say they found in his van the other day?'

'Nothing. Hold on, that's not quite right. Fruit.'

'What sort of fruit?'

'Can't really remember. Bananas, I think. And donuts. Makes me peckish just thinking about them.'

Jackpot. It all fell neatly into place. 'Call your man and tell him to stop Danny and search his van again, and not let him go until we get there.'

'Are you out of your mind? They can't search someone on a whim. There are rules. What do you think they're going to find?'

'Just what I would expect.'

'Great, another one of your revelatory hunches. You'd better be right, or I'm looking at an uncomfortable session in the Super's office.'

'Given all the transgressions you've committed so far, what's another one?' She winked, knowing he wouldn't be able to refuse.

* * *

On Flask Walk, PC George Harding swore fruitily as he stepped in a freshly laid dog souvenir. It was past two o'clock, but the hangover hadn't yet lifted. He'd made the mistake of agreeing to go 'for one' on a Sunday night, to wet the baby's head – couldn't turn down an old friend who was desperate to escape the man-repelling maternity ward. It turned into more than a few; they couldn't even remember getting home. He took a slug of warm Lucozade and knocked on the door.

'Is that your van outside?' Harding said with the best air of authority he could muster under the fraught circumstances.

Danny stood in the doorway, not best pleased at the interruption of his tea break. 'Yeah, so what?' A glimmer of recognition lit on his face. 'Are you the one who pulled me over the other day? I swear, I've had it up to here with you lot. Police harassment this is. I'll be putting in a complaint.'

Lucia and Carliss arrived just as Harding had finished jumping through the legal hoops. Danny had turned bright red and was protesting at the perceived flagrant violation of his human rights. Setting eyes on her made him all the more incensed. 'You? What are you doing here?'

A small crowd had started to gather on the other side of a pavement, thankful for the impromptu entertainment. Lucia peered through the open front door. On the passenger seat sat an innocuous supermarket bag. 'There it is. Have a look inside.' Lucia pointed at the bag.

Carliss nodded to the PC, who took charge of the item. 'Bananas and donuts. What shall I do with them, Guv?' asked Harding, looking distinctly peaky as the sight of food wasn't doing much for his already fragile constitution.

Danny stood frozen, white as the van itself.

'Take a look at this.' Lucia pulled out a banana. Close up, it was a lurid, shiny shade of green. 'It's made of resin.' It looked convincing enough from a distance. She ripped it open to reveal a packet of white powder tightly wrapped in clingfilm. 'No prizes for guessing what this might be.'

'I'll be…' Harding couldn't believe his eyes. 'Coke. You sneaky sod. Thought you'd get away with it.'

Carliss turned to Lucia. 'How did you know?'

'I remembered something I'd watched on TV on Colombian drug smugglers. I'm guessing Danny had done his research. He's smarter than he looks.'

'Not smart enough. Deal with him, Harding, and fill me in later. He'll have a base somewhere, and a stomping ground.'

'I'm pretty certain he's dealing it at the Red Lion,' said Lucia. She remembered the glazed eyes and erratic behaviour of the customers – it all made sense now.

'The pub? That would add up. Hold on, isn't that where Adam Corcoran drinks?'

'Yes, and I bet we've just found out who supplies him.'

'I'll bring Adam in. Should have done it a long time ago. I should have known he's not to be trusted,' Carliss said.

'Hold your horses.' She couldn't have Adam dragged down to the station for questioning – it would ruin her plan. 'Sure, possession is a crime, dealing is a crime, but they're not the crimes we're concerned with. They've got nothing to do with the murder. We already knew Adam was doing drugs, and now we've nailed Danny for it. We need to move on.'

Carliss tapped his foot impatiently.

'Look, I need to talk to you.' She watched PC Harding drive off. 'Not here on the street – somewhere more private. Let's go to my place.'

Grudgingly, he followed her. She walked briskly up the hill and crossed the road with total disregard for her safety – a boxy SUV beeped angrily as she ran in front of it. Carliss swore under his breath and waited at the traffic lights.

'Keep up.' She unlocked the front door and headed upstairs. The flat smelled freshly cleaned, and there were flowers on the kitchen table – showy yellow roses. She threw off her waxed raincoat. The after-effects of the daytime champagne hadn't fully worn off, so she made a pot of strong coffee. 'I've been turning over something you told me about Emilia. The man who was calling her – Stewart Ross. I think I know who he is.'

'Oh?' replied Carliss with surprise in his voice. 'I must admit I'd forgotten all about it.'

'It's Adam.' She was very pleased with herself at this deduction.

'How does that work?'

'Stewart's his middle name. And Ross is his mother's maiden name. All publicly available information.' She hoped he took it as a pointed comment about his reluctance to engage with technology, which it was.

'Hmm. Interesting theory. Won't know for sure unless we ring that number and he picks up. Assuming you're right, why would she need to hide his real identity?'

Lucia couldn't believe he was actually asking the question. 'Really? You haven't worked it out?'

'Worked out what?'

'They must be having an affair, obviously. Why else would she be so cagey about his name and the phone call?' It made sense, even though she knew it was mere speculation at this stage. Even she was beginning to worry that they still didn't have a single shred of concrete evidence, but that wasn't going to stop her.

'If they're having an affair, does this mean he cut her in, like he did with the housekeeper?'

'Perhaps. She might not know about the inheritance. If the police asked me, I'd flatly deny it.'

'No harm in asking.' He checked his watch. 'I wonder if she's hanging around Beatrice Hall. If I didn't know better, I'd be minded to grill the three of them. They must have plotted killing her – there's too much money at stake to miss the opportunity.'

Chapter 29

The key turned in the door. Lucia had feared the locks might have been changed, though she had only been away for a few days. The place was eerily quiet. They tiptoed down to the kitchen. A few dishes sat obediently on the drying rack, suggesting that Adam might have dropped in for a meal. It looked tidy, and as grim as ever.

'Let's try the library.' Lucia had a sense that they weren't alone. If the creaking steps gave them away, there was no evidence of any response. She tentatively opened one of the tall doors, expecting she had been mistaken.

Behind the noticeably less cluttered desk sat Emilia, leaning into the high-backed chair as if she naturally belonged there. For a split second, before facial recognition kicked in, Lucia thought it was the Professor. The grey dress, the butterfly brooch – it was an unsettling déjà vu. The blonde hair was tied up in a severe bun, and the eyes had abandoned their limpid charm.

'Lucia. What a surprise. I wasn't expecting anyone. Oh, and Inspector Carliss. To what do I owe this pleasure?' She didn't stand up to greet them. They were on her turf.

Carliss waded straight in. 'I've got a question for you, Miss Poole. Are you and Adam romantically involved?'

Emilia laughed. When she was done, her eyes looked as steely as those of the Professor, as Lucia could clearly remember from the last time she was in the library. 'What a sweet way of describing it, Inspector. And what if we are?'

'Can you please answer the question?'

Lucia was furious that she had them both on the back foot – two school children up before the headteacher, waiting to be reprimanded.

Emilia shrugged indifferently. 'Yes, I'm sleeping with Adam. What's that got to do with anything?'

'Did you know that he stands to inherit Beatrice Hall?' continued Carliss.

'No, I had no idea.' She looked maddeningly blank.

'Did you know the Professor was planning to change her will and disinherit him before she died?'

'It's the first I've heard of this will.' No hoped-for flash of admission across her serene face – not as much as a blink.

'He didn't confide in you, even though you're in a relationship?'

She tilted her head forward with contempt. 'Just because I go to bed with him occasionally doesn't make me his agony aunt, Inspector.'

Lucia would have dearly liked to step in, but she bit her tongue and hoped the policeman would move on to a more effective line of questioning.

'Does the name Stewart Ross mean anything to you, Miss Poole?' he carried on hopefully, trying in vain to deliver the killer blow.

Instead of being ruffled, Emilia smiled. 'It's Adam. We didn't want the Professor knowing about our affair. It's unlikely she would have approved – I was here as her employee, after all. Full marks for working it out, Inspector, though I suspect you might have had a little help.' This she addressed pointedly at Lucia.

'Lovely brooch,' retorted Lucia.

'Ah, this. It was on the desk when I came in. I thought I'd try it on – I must have forgotten to take it off. Not really my style.' She unhooked it gently off her dress and flicked it to one side.

'What are you doing in the library anyway?' asked Carliss. Lucia could see he was running out of ideas.

'I'm sorting through the Professor's papers. It would be a shame for all of this work to go to waste. Once I've filed everything, I'm planning to donate it to the Collaborative Mathematical Society. It's what she would have wanted. Now, if you don't mind, I'd like to get on with it.' She went back to her papers, shutting out the unwanted visitors.

Powerless, they shuffled back downstairs.

'What did you make of that, Lucia?'

'I don't know what to think any more. She clearly couldn't care less about Adam. Whether she was using him to get to the inheritance, I don't know. She and her employer spent practically every waking hour together. It's plausible that the will would have been mentioned at some point.'

'I don't know what it is about that woman – she throws me every time. If one of my sergeants had been that cack-handed with an interview, I would have sent them packing.'

The humiliation stung, and Lucia could see it. 'She didn't waste any time moving in to take the Professor's place. I wonder what she's planning to do next. Not elope with Adam, that's for sure. She knows she's being watched now.'

They stood on the steps outside, and Carliss lit a cigarette. 'I'd sworn your mate Nina's tempting Sobranies would be the last, but I'm stressed,' he explained apologetically. 'Want one?'

'No, thanks. They don't help.'

He shrugged with resignation. 'I know they don't. I just wish I could give them up.'

'We all have our vices.' Lucia's sat quietly in a smooth envelope in her bedroom, waiting to be consumed as required.

'What's yours? White Burgundy doesn't count, by the way.'

'You rumbled me. That's the only one.' She was fully aware of the irony engendered by the earlier drugs bust. 'I wouldn't mind an early night. I'll let you know if I hear back from Nina. And I'll go back to work at Beatrice Hall tomorrow. That way I can keep close tabs on Emilia.'

'Early night it is then.'

Lucia ambled back up Hampstead High Street. The rush hour was long gone, and the shop shutters were coming down, one by one, ready for a night's rest. A lone old man nursed a cloudy pint at a table outside a pub even more sterile than the Hampstead Belle. Drugs, sex, money, vengeance, murder – and no closer to finding out how they fitted together. She had begun to question her own judgment. Perhaps Carliss had been right all along, and the rest was a mere distraction.

She sat on her bed, laptop propped on a pillow and a glass of cold wine on the bedside table. She was itching to dig around, but she had already exhausted the information she had on the suspects. Until Nina worked her magic, there was little chance of unearthing anything new. She opened the bedside drawer and looked at the envelope. It wasn't ideal, but it was better than nothing. She needed to relax.

With the alcohol and the ketamine inside her, she soon sank into floating, pleasurable oblivion. Jumbled thoughts coursed through her head. For no particular reason, she remembered how Carliss had her pegged as a rich Home Counties girl. She pictured what she would say to him: 'My mum brought me up on her own. She had me young, and my dad legged it as soon as she told him she was pregnant. We lived in a small council flat up in Hampstead. She was a dinner lady at the local primary school. Every Saturday we'd go to the library. It was my special treat – two or three books to see me through the week. I was bright, so I went to university. She wanted me to be a lawyer, to have a profession and be on my own two feet.'

As the stupor was gradually fading into light-headedness, Lucia heard the ring of her phone. She blinked and stared at the blurry screen. Five missed calls. She didn't trust herself not to drop it, so she put it on speaker and stared at it, waiting to come back to consciousness.

'Lucia, you won't believe this. Adam's dead.'

Chapter 30

When she arrived early the following day, as hastily arranged with the inspector, Lucia found Beatrice Hall transformed. She had been warned not to bother bringing her van – every single space outside the house was taken up by police vehicles. The outer gate had been left open and kept bashing into the brick wall with a mournful creak. The place seethed with faceless boiler suits photographing, measuring, taking samples. The body had been removed. In the entrance hall, Carliss paced up and down nervously, shouting instructions on his phone. She closed the doors behind her and waited for him to finish, not wanting to interrupt.

He gave out a heavy, exhausted sigh – it had been a long night. His hair looked in need of a good brush. 'Ah, good, you're here. It's absolute mayhem. I've had to sell my soul to get the PM fast-tracked. He had enough cocaine in him for several heart attacks. Of course, it helped that it had been laced with 1080.'

'Poison?'

'No question about it. The inside of his nose was caked in the stuff. Mrs Byrne found him in his room last night and raised the alarm. They were meant to have dinner together in the kitchen, but he didn't turn up.'

Lucia was glad she'd rationed her ketamine intake the night before. The situation required a clear head. 'But the tin of poison was removed after the Professor's death. Where did the new batch come from?'

'Doesn't have to be a new batch. He could have kept some back,' said the policeman.

'Are you saying he killed himself?'

'It's not out of the question. Could have been intentional, could have been an accident. Maybe he couldn't live with the guilt of what he'd done or didn't fancy spending the rest of his life behind bars.' He paused for a moment, considering the possibilities. 'There's a third option. If he didn't do himself in, anyone could have helped themselves to the stuff while it lived under the sink. Including someone who dropped by for occasional jobs.'

The comment was too specific for her to miss. 'Whom do you have in mind?'

'Danny Garrett. We've got him down at the station. He fessed up to intending to sell the stash of cocaine, and to supplying Adam. Since he was in a sharing mood, he also admitted to wrecking your van, though criminal damage is the least of his troubles right now. Apparently, the dead bloke wasn't paying his debts, what with his getting sacked.'

Lucia remembered the evening at the pub with Becky and Leila, and the heated argument that Adam was having on the phone. 'OK, Danny was owed money. That doesn't make him a killer. In fact, dispatching Adam would guarantee he would never get paid.'

'True. But listen to this: Adam kept telling Danny he wanted to get clean. What if he was minded to expose Danny's drugs racket? That would give Danny a good motive for murder. He knew the house – he says he's been doing odd jobs at the Hall for years. He could have easily got hold of the 1080 from under the kitchen sink. I like him for it. Sometimes the easy solution is the right one, Lucia.'

She smiled and tapped her forehead. How could she have been so naïve? 'I know why Adam gave me the job.'

'Why is that?'

'So that he wouldn't be pressured into giving it to Danny. Anyone but him. Danny must have figured out pretty quickly that the Professor was the only source of cash. He may look like a brainless brute, but he's not daft. If Adam agreed to pay him a suitably inflated price for the decorating, that's the drugs debt written off. Except Adam didn't want him anywhere near the house. No wonder he thought I was a godsend, turning up out of the blue asking for the work. And that's what made Danny so angry that he defaced my van.'

'That certainly adds up. I've finally got a good feeling about this whole sorry affair. Adam killed the old bird, and now he's dead himself. Danny goes down for his murder. Case closed. We all go home.' He crossed his arms resolutely.

Lucia's expression made it patently clear that she wasn't going to indulge him. 'I don't buy it. Danny's a scumbag and a drug dealer, but to go from that to killing a person is a touch far-fetched. Besides, what are you going to do when you search his house and van, and you don't find any traces of 1080? I'd stick with the drugs charges if I were you.'

'OK, so we haven't filled in all the gaps yet. But if he's done as much as look at that poison, we'll get him, don't you worry. The Super wants me to close this case and move on – too many resources spent running around pretending I'm Poirot, she said. I know I've broken just about every rule in the book, but even I can't keep this circus going any longer.'

'When are you speaking to the other suspects?'

'Any time now. Danny's being covered. That only leaves Emilia and Mrs Byrne.'

'What about Glover?'

'What about him? He wasn't anywhere near the house.'

'Don't you think it's worth at least a phone call? To see how he reacts to the news.'

The policeman huffed impatiently. 'I'm starting to see where the Super is coming from. You're a drain on the public purse, Miss Steer.'

'But you'll ring him?'

'Yes, OK, just to get you off my back. Now scoot off. I've got some statements to take.'

Lucia stood still. 'There's no way I'm going anywhere. Nina's on her way. You're going to tell them she's your new DS, and I'm helping you with your enquiries. We're sitting in on the interviews.'

'You must be joking. I'm not having you two compromise my investigation. I'm not one for formalities, but this really takes the biscuit.'

'Suit yourself if that's how you want it. But remember one thing – you haven't got a shred of evidence against Danny Garrett. An unsolved case is going to be a bigger drain on your resources than letting us in.' It was her turn to cross her arms and stare at him defiantly.

'OK. But not a peep from either of you. I'm doing all the talking,' he finally replied, cornered and defeated by her determination.

'Deal,' said Lucia, wholly unconcerned about the possible consequences of his transgressions, just as her phone rang. Nina was outside. She had already been prepped to turn up in character before Lucia had even asked the inspector.

Mrs Byrne sat on the threadbare drawing room sofa, fidgeting with her hands in her lap. Nina, Lucia and DCI Carliss occupied the remaining armchairs, directly facing her. Nina looked the part – no make-up, severe expression, and a flammable navy-blue trouser suit. She clutched her pad and pen officiously. Lucia looked as sympathetic as could be.

Carliss opened gingerly. 'Mrs Byrne, I appreciate this is very distressing, but it would be useful to get the facts while they're still fresh in your mind. Can you take me through Adam's movements yesterday?'

Mrs Byrne had aged ten years since Lucia last saw her. Her eyes were puffy and red. 'Yes, of course. I'll do my best to help. He… Adam was out for most of the day. He came back around five – I was having a cup of tea in the kitchen. He joined me, and said he'd be around for dinner. We haven't seen each other much of late, and I was looking forward to a bit of company.' She looked like she was about to burst into tears.

Nina whipped a box of tissues from her handbag and offered it to the housekeeper.

'I'm sorry. First the Professor, and now this…' Mrs Byrne gathered herself together as best she could. 'I said I'd have dinner ready for seven. He went up to his room, and I didn't hear anything after that. Next thing I know, I'm waiting and waiting. When I went up, it was just gone half past. He was lying on his bed. I thought he'd fallen asleep at first, but then I got closer.' Her voice trembled. 'His eyes and mouth were wide open, and that… stuff was on his bedside table. Oh, if only I'd known. I could have helped him. Persuaded him to get treatment. I let him die.' Her resolve not to cry had been broken; she was wailing and rocking backwards and forwards, head buried in her hands.

Nina got out of her armchair and sat down gently next to the woman for comfort. 'Mrs Byrne, it's not your fault. Drug addiction is a tragic and complex business. We want to help, but we're powerless. If he didn't want to give it up, there was nothing that you or anyone else could have done. Don't blame yourself.'

'What time did Adam go upstairs, Mrs Byrne?' continued Carliss.

The housekeeper blew her nose loudly and looked a little restored. 'Must have been sixish, or a little earlier. I don't honestly know.'

'Was Adam himself? Did he seem out of sorts in any way?'

'No, he was fine. If anything, more talkative than I'd seen him in ages. You don't think… he did it on purpose?' Mrs Byrne let out another sob. 'Maybe he took an overdose because he couldn't live with himself anymore. Was that it?'

'We don't know for certain, but we need to consider all angles.'

The trio had decided it was best she should labour under the impression that Adam's death had been the result of a cocaine overdose. The poison would be kept out of it, for now at least.

'Thank you. And can you tell me your movements yesterday? Just routine, you understand.'

'I got up at six thirty, as usual, and did a little light cleaning. There's not much, now it's only me and… well, only me in the house. Emilia arrived around nine thirty and went upstairs. So good of her, to soldier on with all that dusty paperwork. She came down to the garden at lunchtime for a cuppa. She ate the sandwich she'd brought with her and went back upstairs. She left shortly before Adam arrived – half past four or so.'

'Was she in the library the rest of the time?'

'Well, yes, I suppose she would have been. I was cleaning the kitchen. I didn't hear any doors open or close, but I did have the hoover on for a while. After lunch, I went to tackle the gardening.'

'So, you were outside until Adam arrived?'

'Yes. Emilia dropped by to say she was going. She must have got bored of sitting in that horrid room all day.'

If that's what she did, thought Lucia. Emilia could have roamed the house at her leisure, for all Mrs Byrne knew.

'Was there anyone else in the house at any point during the day?' asked the policeman.

'No, not that day.' She stopped to think. 'Dr Glover popped in a couple of times last week. Helping Emilia with the Professor's paperwork, he was. Very kind of him.'

'That's it for now, Mrs Byrne. Thank you for your time.'

When the door was firmly shut behind her, Lucia burst out. 'That man didn't commit suicide.'

'You don't think it was Mrs Byrne?' asked Carliss. 'Though I can't imagine why she would want Adam dead.'

'No, that seems unlikely. This business of Emilia being in the house, and Dr Glover dropping in – all very bizarre.' Lucia wondered what they found so fascinating about the Professor's papers.

'I'm dying to meet this elusive being at last.' Nina tidied up the tissues and readied herself for the next round.

Carliss went to fetch Emilia, who had been instructed to wait in the entrance hall until summoned. She had evidently dressed for a man's eyes – the finely knitted green wool dress fitted her like a glove. She hadn't banked on having female company, not that she flinched when she saw the two. The only giveaways were her frosty manner and the absence of eye contact with anyone but the policeman.

'I didn't expect to see you again so soon, Inspector. I see you've brought back-up.' Her lips narrowed sarcastically as she crossed her shapely ankles, knowing that Carliss was struggling to keep his eyes focused on her face.

'Yes. This is – erm – this is DS Chanler. Miss Steer is kindly helping us with our enquiries,' the inspector stuttered, somewhat flustered.

Lucia felt for him – he had to make something up on the spot to justify Nina's presence as well as try to regain some ground.

'Miss Poole, I'm fully aware these are very unpleasant circumstances, so I'll keep my questions as brief as possible. Could you tell me your whereabouts yesterday?' Carliss said, consulting his notebook for comfort.

'I arrived at nine thirty, as usual, and went straight upstairs. I worked until lunch when I went down to the garden and chatted to Mrs Byrne. After that I carried on working until half past four, when I left. Does that suit your purposes?'

'You didn't see Adam while you were here?'

'No.'

'And you were here last week?'

'Yes, on the same schedule.'

Lucia noticed that, unlike the housekeeper, Emilia's eyes were dry and if anything, she looked bored.

'Forgive me, Miss Poole, but you don't seem particularly affected by your boyfriend's death,' continued Carliss.

Emilia shot him a condescending look. 'How would you know how I feel, Inspector? Just because I'm not making a song and dance about his demise doesn't mean it isn't upsetting. In any case, he wasn't my boyfriend. It was a casual relationship.'

Carliss squirmed in his seat. 'How did he seem to you generally? Was anything concerning him?'

'You mean, apart from the fact he had a cocaine habit? He was an addict. He wanted to stop, but he couldn't. He was always on edge – overtired and paranoid. I gather it doesn't exactly aid sleep. He wasn't any worse than normal if that's what you're asking.'

She looked out of the window, and Lucia sensed she was more affected than she wanted to let on. Perhaps under the flinty exterior she did have a heart after all.

After a brief pause, Emilia continued. 'I knew it would be the death of him. Addicts are selfish. He didn't listen to me, or anyone else.' Her searching gaze suddenly fixed on

Nina, who kept her head down and carried on taking copious notes, hoping she wasn't attracting any attention.

'I understand Dr Glover has been lending you a hand with the Professor's papers. Very good of him to offer,' noted the policeman.

She smiled benignly. 'Yes, he's been a great help. I think he takes a personal interest in her research – a bit of a boffin in that respect. It all looks terribly dull to me, I'm afraid. That Society of hers is welcome to all of it.'

Carliss was at a loss. 'Thank you, Miss Poole. You're free to go.'

They breathed a collective sigh of relief.

'What a woman,' exclaimed Nina. 'And I thought Mater was terrifying.'

'What she saw in Adam is beyond me. Still, we all have our physiological needs, and he wasn't likely to turn her down,' opined Lucia.

'Still want me to call the Doc? I know what he's going to say – same as what Emilia's just told us,' intervened Carliss.

'There's no harm in trying. And put him on speakerphone. We don't want to miss out.' Lucia wanted to hear his voice for herself.

By a stroke of luck, Dr Glover was between patients. Carliss was immediately warned that he had precisely five minutes of the GP's precious time.

'That should be plenty, Dr Glover. I have some very unpleasant news, I'm afraid, in case you haven't heard already. Adam Corcoran was found dead last night.'

The voice on the other end didn't hesitate. 'Yes, I know. Emilia rang me earlier. Awful business.'

'I understand you were recently at Beatrice Hall. What was the purpose of your visit?'

'I offered to help Emilia with tidying up the Professor's library. It's all going to the Collaborative Mathematical Society, and she could have done with some assistance.

What has this got to do with Adam's death?' The voice had an unmistakable tinge of exasperation.

'I'm simply trying to ascertain the movements of everyone who visited Beatrice Hall over the past week. Were you there yesterday?'

'No, I had back-to-back appointments so couldn't make it. Is there anything else, Inspector? I have a patient waiting.'

'Thank you, Dr Glover, you've been most helpful.'

Carliss put the phone down and scratched his head. 'Traipsing around the place as they've been, either of these two could have cut Adam's coke with poison. The part I'm struggling with is motive, which takes me back to my original assessment – it was most likely self-inflicted.'

Lucia opened her mouth to counteract what to her was an inexcusably flippant verdict, when Nina's phone started vibrating like an angry wasp.

'It's Mother.'

Bar a few acquiescing sounds, the short conversation was mostly one-sided. Nina swept up her belongings and made for the door. 'We need to go. She's meeting us at my place in half an hour.'

'What's this about? I'm in no mood for boozing in Belgravia, not with a fresh dead body on the cards,' Carliss interrupted impatiently.

'She can't tell me on the phone. I can only assume she's dug up something good. Hurry up – you don't want to face her if you're late.'

Chapter 31

After a twenty-minute rollercoaster ride to rival Lucia's dangerous driving, the taxi spat them out at Lygon Place. They would have liked a little time to settle the contents of their stomachs, but they had barely taken their coats off when the doorbell rang.

'Mater. Lovely to see you. You've kept us all in suspense.'

From the doorway, Virginia Lexington's hazel eyes scanned the company her daughter was keeping and appeared to deem it satisfactory. The precision-cut cap of grey hair, wide-legged trousers and mannish shirt made for redoubtable armour. 'Lucia, my darling. It's been too long.' They embraced warmly.

Nina ushered them into the house and made the requisite introductions. 'Detective Chief Inspector Carliss, the SIO for Professor Kiseleva's death. My mother, Virginia Lexington.'

'Pleased to meet you, ma'am,' Carliss said, at a loss as to how to address her.

'Virginia, please. I'm retired – all this business of titles is behind me.' She dismissed him with a haughty glance and marched decisively into the drawing room, which she proceeded to assess with an unequivocal scrunch of the nose. It was plain that her progeny's taste in interiors didn't pass muster.

Carliss tiptoed behind the group and sat down as far away from her as possible.

'Tea?' offered Nina.

Lucia was amused by the detective's ill-concealed unease – it was a common enough reaction to Virginia Lexington's presence. She must have reminded him too much of the Super. Lucia and Nina were used to the style of silent dressing-down and didn't take it to heart.

'No time for small talk, dear child. Since I've got your undivided attention, I'll crack on. That chap Glover you had me look into has given me no end of trouble. I've pulled more strings than Jim Henson, but I have managed to deliver. He was in Belarus – or Byelorussia, as it then was – from 1981 to 1983. All very neat and above board – the British Council had recently set up an educational exchange programme for British doctors to travel out there and vice versa. Needless to say, Glover's military background made him the perfect choice.' Virginia paused and looked suspiciously around the room. 'Sorry. Even in retirement, being listened to remains an occupational hazard. That's why I couldn't impart the information on the phone.'

'I'm sure we're perfectly safe here, Mater.'

'Yes, I should think so. People can't be falling over each other to manipulate the market in sprats.'

Lucia suppressed a smile. Although Virginia Lexington was very fond of her son-in-law, she couldn't resist being amused at his line of work. She herself was from Nottinghamshire farming stock. Though she had married Guy Lexington – renowned Cambridge historian and heir to Lexington Hall – she had risen up in the diplomatic service by sheer determination and hard work, so the jibe was fairly innocent.

Virginia nodded pensively. 'Of course, swapping knowledge about infection control wasn't the real reason for Dr Glover's presence at that end of Europe. We had a double agent in Minsk, a secretary at the ministry of health. They met under the guise that she was assisting him with his work. I don't know her name. What I do know is that it became more than a purely professional relationship. London was getting rather antsy – there were even rumours of an engagement. Before they could reprimand him, the woman was found dead in her flat. The case was rapidly closed as suicide – the bullet went cleanly through her temple, and the gun was in her hand. Naturally, London didn't buy it, and he was withdrawn immediately. It turns out the Belarusians had someone with an eye on her all along – a false defector, who gained her confidence and was only known as Clytemnestra. One can only assume she was a woman. And there the thread ends, I'm afraid.'

'And the Professor?' Carliss asked.

'Nothing on that front beyond what you already know from Nina. Either my sources aren't all they're cracked up to be, or she's covered her tracks impeccably.'

Lucia's expression suggested she was cooking something up. 'Clytemnestra, you said?' She rummaged around in her bag and produced an object which she placed on the white marble coffee table. 'Does anyone know what this is?'

Apart from Nina, they gathered around with quizzical looks.

'Is this a trick question?' asked Virginia, somewhat confused.

'It's a jazzy leafwing. The Latin name is *Hypna clytemnestra*,' explained Lucia, waiting for a reaction.

Carliss recognized the black and white butterfly-shaped brooch. 'Emilia was wearing it when we spoke to her in the library. She said it belonged to her employer. How did you get it?' he asked.

'I swiped it earlier. I knew I'd seen it on the Professor when I first met her. It struck me as too peculiar a piece not to have special significance. I looked it up, but the name meant nothing to me until now.' Getting hold of the piece of jewellery had been childishly easy. All it took was a speedy incursion upstairs before sitting down with Mrs Byrne, while the inspector had nipped to the facilities and Nina kept watch.

'Lucia, are you suggesting the Professor is Clytemnestra?' asked Virginia with an impressed look on her face.

'It could be a long shot, but there's no such thing as a coincidence, as the inspector is probably sick of hearing me say.'

'So unusual.' Nina picked up the brooch gingerly and turned it over. The underside was matt gold, which made the masterfully engraved inscription all the more striking. 'This must be Belarusian. My language skills are somewhat rusty.' She strained to make sense of the words.

'How come you speak it?' asked Carliss.

'I read Russian at university. The two are not identical, of course, but there are sufficient similarities between them. I believe the writing says: "For services rendered".' The delicate object sat innocently in Nina's outstretched palm. 'I think we can extrapolate what sort of services they might be. The code name speaks for itself.'

'The scheming murderess with the mind of a man,' said the policeman.

'I wouldn't have guessed you were a fan of ancient Greek tragedy, Inspector.'

'We're not all PC Plod, you know. Though I never guessed an evening seeing the Oresteia at the National Theatre would ever be directly relevant to my work. But this doesn't mean anything for our case. We've got no proof that Glover knew the Professor was the one who got his lady friend killed.'

'True, but it makes for a damn good motive, don't you think?' replied Lucia. 'His fiancée was killed by a double agent. That's not something he would have easily forgotten, even though it was nearly forty years ago. He turns up at Beatrice Hall and sees the brooch – once, twice, until he twigs, like we did, that it's not a mere adornment. He puts two and two together and realizes the woman he's been hunting all this time has been right under his nose all along.'

'Slow down, Miss Marple. This is all fanciful. It's hardly going to wash in the interview room.'

Lucia knew he was right, not that it alleviated her frustration.

'And Adam? Are you saying Glover was responsible for his death as well?' continued the inspector. 'From where I'm standing, the story's getting more fantastical by the minute.'

'Perhaps Adam found out about the Professor's and Glover's shared past. Don't forget he was a forensic accountant, albeit an unemployed one – uncovering secrets would have been his bread and butter,' added Nina.

'You lot are making my head spin. The bottom line is, I can't arrest a man on what you've brought me so far,' protested Carliss.

Virginia tapped her foot impatiently. 'Pleasant as this may be, I'm going to have to leave you to your deliberations. We're going out to dinner, and I've got to drag your father out of the British Library first. He's writing yet another book on medieval churches, as if the world hasn't got plenty already.'

They said their various goodbyes, with Carliss the unfortunate recipient of a crushing handshake, and the depleted team sat back down despondently.

'Look, I'm not saying you're wrong. We just need to get our hands on some real evidence before I can move forward,' said the detective conciliatorily.

Lucia was at that very moment harbouring a niggling doubt. As she reviewed the tableau of the tea party where the Professor had met her end, a particular detail grated. She strained to recall what the inspector had recounted of his first visit to Dr Glover's office. It would come to her, she was sure. For the moment, the more urgent preoccupation lay elsewhere. 'Can we see Adam's post-mortem report?' It was worth a shot, Lucia reasoned, though she knew Carliss was well within his rights to refuse.

To her surprise, he yielded straightaway. 'I've contravened just about everything, so why not?' He threw his arms up in the air despairingly and handed them his phone. He stood up and went to look out of the window. Behind him, the women huddled closely together, scrolling through the pages.

'What are you hoping to find?' he finally asked, exasperated. 'I've gone through that report with a fine-tooth comb.'

'Nothing in particular. I just want to make sure we haven't missed any important details.' The writing was tiny, and Lucia struggled to follow. 'Hang on, what's this?'

Carliss stared at the paragraph in question. 'It just refers back to the contents of his pockets, for completeness. They were empty, apart from one item. Here – "small straw doll – see photo below." It will have been bagged up and checked in at the station. Just one of those random things, I suppose.'

He took possession of the phone and was about to replace it in his pocket when Nina interrupted. 'Let me have a closer look at that picture.'

To anyone else's eyes, the item would have appeared unremarkable – a tiny, weaved doll in some sort of national dress, the kind that littered souvenir shops at popular holiday destinations all over the world. It had a jolly little face, with round green eyes and bright red lips, topped with a white flower headdress.

To Nina, the toy clearly meant much more. She peered more closely at the screen, examining the tightly bound skirt and fingerless hands. 'It's flax, not straw. It looks like a traditional Belarusian *lialka* – a doll given to young children as an amulet for good luck.'

She magnified the picture until she could make out the spindly writing embroidered on the apron and read out the single word: "Emilia".

Chapter 32

The three exchanged incredulous looks.

DCI Carliss broke the silence. 'I think we need to crank it up a notch, see where she's come from. We've got woefully little on the woman.' He got up abruptly and went to retrieve his overcoat. 'I'm going back to the station. I'll let you know when I've got more.'

As soon as he was out of earshot, Lucia turned to her friend. 'He feels bad for not taking a closer look at her past earlier. It's that schoolgirl charm – men can't help but fall for it.'

For the next few days, life settled into a false semblance of normality. With Beatrice Hall irredeemably out of bounds, Lucia was at a loss. She had no other work lined up – the investigation had swallowed up her entire existence. There was no word from Margaret, who had solemnly promised – and duly failed – to get in touch over the proposed rehaul of the Walkers' residence.

At Nina's insistence, Lucia was put up in the Chanlers' spare room in Belgravia while the two friends struggled to make sense of the recent tragedies. To cheer them up, Walter had suggested a trip up north to Lexington Hall.

They were busy packing up the car when Lucia's phone rang.

'I'm sorry for going AWOL. We've been working day and night to get to the bottom of this. Can I come over?' Carliss's voice sounded half adrenaline, half fatigue.

As Lucia apologetically explained the change of plan, Walter turned to his wife with a knowing smile. 'I know what you're like, darling. You two go ahead and catch your murderer, I'll be just fine drinking whisky in front of the fire with your father.'

With Walter on the road, the women went back into the house and waited for the bell to ring. It didn't take long. Nina opened the door to an exceptionally dishevelled detective, even by his standards. The three-day stubble and dark circles under his eyes, coupled with the state of his clothes, strongly suggested he had been surviving on black coffee and might not have left the office at all.

'You look in dire need of a square meal and a bath. Can I tempt you, Inspector? You look about the same size as Walter. I'm sure he'd be more than happy to lend you something clean to wear,' offered Nina.

'Thanks, but I'm fine.'

Lucia could see he wasn't fine at all – he was tormented by what might have been the avoidable death of Adam Corcoran, and it pained her. 'Tell us everything, from the beginning.' She led him gently to the sofa.

He had his rucksack with him, the one that only got aired when there was serious business at play. Out of it emerged a folder with painstakingly labelled tabs. He opened it at the first page and began. 'I had this sitting on my desk all along and didn't give it a second thought. Tell me what you see – or rather, what strikes you.' It was a copy of Emilia's passport.

'Vera Emilia Poole. She uses her second name then – not unheard of. Born on the 21st of December 1982 in Brest.' Lucia paused to think. 'I suppose that's not unusual.

Her parents must have travelled a lot, or they could have been living in France at the time.'

She was about to carry on when the policeman interrupted her. He had a haunted look on his face. 'And there's the error, staring us right in the face. My error. She was born in Brest, Belarus, not Brest, France. I stared at this wretched page until the words were a blur, and then I remembered something I learned at school a long time ago. The Treaty of Brest-Litovsk.'

'The end of Russia's First World War,' said Nina.

'From then on, I didn't stop until I tracked her down. The poor DS that got lumbered with me at the station really did draw the short straw – it's been a hell of a time. It turns out that Richard and Christine Poole weren't her real parents. She's adopted.'

'From Belarus, sure,' Lucia interjected. 'But what's this got to do with the Professor?'

'Oh, it gets better.' Carliss turned the page. 'Her entry in the Adopted Children Register confirms her country of birth. There's only one orphanage in Brest where she could have come from, so we roped in a translator and got to work. A hell of a lot of phone calls later, she finds out it closed in 1992, so we're back to square one. Cue some more prodding, lateral thinking, hours of waiting, you name it, we did it, and bingo – we get sent Emilia's papers from the Brest city archive.' He stopped for a moment to catch his breath and wipe beads of sweat from his forehead.

'I'll get you a glass of water,' said Nina. 'And slow down – I don't want you on my conscience.'

Oblivious to the dark humour, Carliss gulped the water down in one go and clutched his well-thumbed folder. 'Born Vera Emilia Polyakova to Nadzeya Polyakova. Father unknown. The child was registered in the orphanage records when she was five weeks old. After that, nothing, until the adoption – the first, or attempted adoption, I should say, by someone called Olga Galina, in

February 1983. I can't find any trace of the reason it fell through. The second adoption, later that year, was by Richard and Christine Poole, who took the baby back to the UK with them – and thus Emilia Poole was born.'

'But who is Olga Galina?' asked Lucia. 'The name means nothing.'

'I haven't got as far as that. The DS and I ran out of steam,' admitted the inspector. 'I was hoping you two can help.'

Nina ran to fetch her laptop. They sat in a circle on the floor and got to work. Hours passed in a frenzied haze. Bottles of wine were consumed, a takeaway meal was hastily eaten and the light streaming in grew dimmer and dimmer. The screen started hurting their eyes before they noticed it was dark and switched on the sumptuous chandelier. That Olga Galina happened to be the name of a famous Russian opera singer did little to help the search.

As the clock on the mantelpiece struck one, they were on the verge of calling it a night, when Nina gave a shrill cry. 'Look at this.'

The black and white photograph showed a group of people awkwardly clumped together against the background of a sprawling blackboard covered in equations. Allowing for minimal variations by gender, they were dressed in stern dark suits and boxy dresses. The Cyrillic writing at the bottom was faded to only just short of illegible.

'Faculty of Applied Mathematics, Belarus State University, 1981,' read out Nina. 'And look at the first name on the list – Dr Olga Galina.'

The first person from the left was a woman in her late thirties or early forties, whose light attire stood out in the sea of gloomy blacks and dark greys. As the picture was magnified, they were able to make out a dark butterfly-shaped brooch on her lapel. Though forty years younger, the face was unmistakably that of the woman known as Professor Alla Kiseleva – the almond-shaped eyes framed by a wavy bob, the high cheekbones, the faintly disdainful expression on her lips. It matched the photo on the unmarked file that Nina had dug up. Lucia sat back and shuddered at the magnitude of their discovery.

'Tell me I'm not hallucinating. It's her, isn't it?' said Carliss, as if he no longer trusted his own judgement.

'It's definitely her,' muttered Nina.

'If the Professor is Olga Galina, did Emilia know that her employer nearly became her adoptive mother? And if Emilia did know, was that worth killing for?' wondered Lucia out loud.

'It certainly was, Lulu. The conditions in those Belarus orphanages were infernal – starving children confined to their cots, widespread abuse…' Nina stopped, unable to continue, and her eyes welled up.

'You were there?' asked Carliss in amazement.

'Yes, as an exchange student – unfortunately, nothing has changed for those poor things since the 1980s. That sort of start to her life, it can't but leave marks.' Nina emptied her glass and started clearing the debris that had accumulated around them.

Lucia pictured Emilia's implacable face, her cold detachment – it all made sense. In the whirlwind of the revelation, they had forgotten one thing. 'If Adam had the doll, he could have found Emilia out, confronted her perhaps. He needed to be eliminated.' She knew full well what the stumbling block would be.

The policeman, despite his exhaustion, didn't wait long to point it out. 'We're back to the same problem we've had before – plenty of motive, not a shred of solid evidence.'

'There has to be something,' reasoned Lucia. 'She must have gone wrong somewhere, like she did with the champagne coupe. Oh, that was brilliant – though the execution wasn't quite perfect.' She racked her brains. 'What else was taken into evidence when your people first searched Beatrice Hall?'

'You mean, after the Professor's… after Olga's death? Oh, I don't even know what to call the woman anymore.' He frowned. 'The crockery and cutlery used for the party. I released them soon after they tested negative for poison – there's only so long we can keep rotting food before it becomes a health and safety hazard.' He rubbed his reddened eyes. 'Oh, and the tin of 1080, obviously.'

Lucia perked up. 'Did they find anything on the tin?'

'Nothing of interest, otherwise we would have known. Only the housekeeper's fingerprints, from whenever she used it last.'

'We need to look at it again. If any physical evidence was left behind, that's where it'll be.' Lucia rose to her feet with fresh determination. She was too tired to remember that it was now the middle of the night.

'Well, it's not going to happen now, that's for sure. We can go down to the station nice and early in the morning, but I think we're clutching at straws. Everything has been processed within an inch of its life,' replied Carliss.

'Let's go to bed. You can sleep here if you like, Inspector, or I can call you a cab.'

'Thanks, Nina, I'll head home. I could do with a hot shower before I face tomorrow's entertainment.' He stood up wearily.

Lucia didn't want to think what would happen if there was nothing to be found in the evidence room. Two unexplained deaths, no arrests and a cunning killer who may well get away unscathed. That wasn't good police work.

Chapter 33

Being a Saturday, Kentish Town Station was conveniently understaffed. The inspector escorted Lucia and Nina into his office and ordered them to stay put. It didn't take long to dig out the tin of sodium fluoroacetate, which he deposited on his desk.

'Here it is. Put some gloves on first.' He gestured to a box next to his computer.

Lucia lifted the tin up to the light and looked carefully all the way around the outside. The metal rim at the bottom had rusted slightly – it had probably been sitting in a damp patch when it used to live under the kitchen sink. She edged the lid open with her fingernails and looked inside. The tin was around two-thirds full. So far, so disappointing.

'Have you got a torch?'

The detective dutifully opened a drawer and fished one out.

The bright light bounced off the interior walls of the tin, until it focused on a spot that broke the otherwise uninterrupted stretch of shiny silver metal.

'What do you think this is?' Lucia said to the policeman.

Carliss peered in. 'I can't tell. Looks like a tiny smudge.'

'Was it mentioned in the report?'

'I can't remember off the top of my head. I'll have to check.' He sat down at his computer, tapping away until he pulled up the document. 'Here it is. Description of the tin, contents, prints… No mention of a smudge.'

Lucia's heart was pounding in her chest. She couldn't allow herself to believe they might have made a breakthrough at last. 'Can you send the tin back for testing?'

'Yes, I suppose I'd better. Strange that they missed it. However, there was no reason to pay much attention to the inside of the tin, beyond testing the contents. All the prints were on the outside, as you would expect. We won't know before Monday at the earliest. I exhausted all my goodwill when I pushed for Adam's overnight PM.'

'In that case, I suggest we all go home and sleep it off,' said Nina. 'We're of no use to anyone in this state.'

Lucia knew she was right – they needed a break. Nina dragged her friend back to Lygon Place and suggested a shopping trip, a cinema outing – anything to take their mind off the case – but was rebutted. Lucia acted as if she was in a trance, watching back-to-back films and waiting for news.

On the Monday, just as the two friends were about to sit down to an early lunch, Lucia's phone rang ominously.

'The results are back. It's foundation.' The detective sounded deflated.

It was hardly a smoking gun, Lucia thought quickly. 'Was there any DNA?'

'None.'

'It must have come straight out of the container, in that case,' she deduced. 'Mrs Byrne doesn't wear any foundation, and neither does Margaret Walker. That leaves only one other.'

'But how do we prove it's Emilia's?' asked Nina. 'Hold on, I know that look, Lulu. You've got a plan.'

‘I do. There’s no time to lose. We need to get to Beatrice Hall.’

Lucia desperately hoped that Emilia would be there now that the police had finished. She still had the house key in her handbag and was grateful she had resisted the impulse to hand it back to Mrs Byrne. This was probably the only chance they had to catch the bold murderer responsible for the deaths of Olga Galina and Adam Corcoran.

‘Oh, and make sure you bring the tin of 1080 with you,’ she instructed Carliss. ‘I’ll explain when we get there.’

* * *

As Lucia unlocked the door, they were met with the dull noise of the hoover – it was coming from the kitchen.

The policeman hesitated. ‘This could go disastrously wrong, Lucia. Are you sure you know what you’re doing?’

‘I know you want me to say yes, but, in truth, I’m not. Have you got a better idea?’ She knew he didn’t.

The inspector followed Lucia to the library, while Nina hid under the staircase. He knocked and didn’t wait for an answer before entering.

‘Inspector. What are you doing here?’ This time Emilia had genuinely been caught unaware. She was emptying the desk drawers, and the floor was covered in sheets of paper. She looked like she had been caught in the act. Her usually mellow eyes flashed with ill-concealed hostility.

‘Miss Poole. There was something I wanted to follow up on if you have a minute.’ He hesitated and coughed. This was the sign to Lucia, stationed outside, who in turn would wave to Nina and then run for cover.

Mrs Byrne’s voice resonated from downstairs. ‘Emilia! Emilia!’

Well done, Nina, that’s a very good impression of the housekeeper, Lucia thought admiringly from her hiding place.

‘Excuse me for a moment, Inspector. That sounds like Mrs Byrne. I shouldn’t be too long,’ Emilia excused herself.

As soon as Emilia disappeared down the kitchen stairs, Lucia bolted out of the nearest spare room and searched around the library for Emilia’s bag. The detective kept watch at the door, his blood pressure through the roof. Nina stayed put under the stairs, her mission accomplished for now.

‘Aha, see?’ Lucia pulled out a tube of foundation. The corner was slightly ripped, and a trickle of the stuff had emerged and run dry. ‘This explains it. Now for part two of the plan.’

As Lucia disappeared back down the corridor, Emilia made her way back up. Carliss picked up his phone and pretended to be engrossed in conversation. When he was sure he was in her line of sight, he put it down and affected an air of intense agitation. ‘I’m sorry, Miss Poole. I’ve just had an urgent call from the station, and I need to be on my way. I’ll catch up with you later if that’s OK.’

Emilia looked both bemused and relieved as he ran down the stairs and out of the front door.

Lucia emerged silently into the corridor and stood at the top of the stairs, where she was sure that Emilia would hear her through the closed library doors. She was so nervous, she felt she might be sick. The plan was reckless, with a high probability of failure.

‘Yes, Inspector, good afternoon. I won’t keep you long, it’s just that you said I should call if I remember anything out of the ordinary. Well, it’s not exactly remembering – I found something. You know the tin of rat poison from under the kitchen sink at Beatrice Hall? Yes, the one that your constable returned just the other day. Well, I happened to be needing some wipes – I’d smudged some paint, you see – and I lifted up the tin to look behind it. That’s when I noticed it. A long, dried up streak running down the side. I’m pretty sure it’s foundation.’ She pretended to listen to the response of her imaginary interlocutor. 'Yes, I understand what you're saying, that they found no DNA on the tin. But this is really important. There's only one woman in this household who wears foundation, and it's not Mrs Byrne. OK, OK, please call me back as soon as you can. I've got the tin. I'll leave it on the windowsill by the front door until someone gets here to collect it.'

She huffed noisily and swore under her breath, though sufficiently loudly to make herself heard, and headed downstairs, taking care to make the steps creak as much as possible. She placed the tin carefully where she said she would and joined Nina under the stairs. They held their breath.

The few minutes that went by felt like hours. At last, the staircase creaked tentatively under soft steps. Once at the bottom, Emilia scanned her surroundings and spotted her target. She breathed, visibly relieved, and headed for the windowsill. They could see she was wearing disposable gloves. She lifted the tin gingerly and held it up to the light.

'What are you doing, Emilia?' said Lucia as she and Nina emerged into full view.

At the sound of Lucia's voice, Carliss, who had been waiting outside the front door, walked back into the house and fixed Emilia with an icy stare.

Emilia froze, and time suddenly stood very still.

'Come to recover the incriminating evidence, have we?' continued the policeman. 'You fell for it hook, line and sinker. For all your brains, you lost, Miss Poole. Or should I say, Miss Polyakova?'

Up until his last comment, there had been nothing but surprise and fear in Emilia's eyes. As she heard her old name, the colour rose sharply in her cheeks. Out of the blue, the shapely mouth was distorted into a bloodcurdling scream as she charged with all her strength at Lucia. Before the others could intervene, Emilia slammed her into the wall and grabbed her by the neck. Lucia felt the shock of the impact as if everything around her had gone quiet. She heard her own skull crack against the hard surface – then, darkness.

Chapter 34

Lucia was conscious, even though she couldn't feel her limbs. The pressure of her weight against a flat, moderately soft surface was the only indication that she was still alive. All she could hear was a monotonous beep. She desperately wanted to open her eyes, but they were wilfully oblivious to the signals from the brain. At last, the darkness lifted to unveil a scenery of flashing machinery and the kind face of a young woman in scrubs looking down at her. The reassuring presence smelt of soap and disinfectant.

'You alright, sweetheart? Didn't want to interrupt your rest. You've got some visitors waiting if you're feeling up to it.' The nurse pointed to the door.

Lucia nodded groggily.

'Don't tire her out, or you'll have me to reckon with,' the nurse half-joked.

DCI Carliss and Nina sat down by her bedside.

'Hi, stranger. Welcome back.' Nina smiled through uncontrollable tears.

'What's with the long faces?' joked Lucia. 'You can't get rid of me that easily.' She knew Nina wasn't a crier, so it had to be serious.

'It's not funny, Lulu. You scared the living daylights out of us.' Her friend leaned forward, her face pale with worry and lack of sleep. 'The doctors couldn't find a brain injury, but they didn't know when you'd wake up, or what state you'd be in. We've been here day and night, waiting for you to come back to the land of the living.'

Lucia winced. Despite the industrial-strength painkillers, the throbbing pain in the back of her head blurred her vision. 'You don't know how happy I am to see you both.'

The inspector stared at her with his sad blue eyes. 'The consultant said we should be prepared for the worst – anything from memory loss, speech difficulties, depression to even personality changes.' His lips spread into a tentative smile. 'You look much the same as before. Mind you, you haven't told me off yet, so maybe you've had a personality change after all,' he joked feebly.

'What happened to Emilia?' Lucia suddenly gasped. As she gradually came to her senses, the recent events began to unfurl in her mind.

'I called for back-up, and she was arrested. She was completely beside herself with rage – it's a while since I've seen anything like it. Uniform had to handcuff her and practically drag her kicking and screaming into the car. You can imagine the circus – apparently the whole street was out watching,' replied the detective.

'Apparently? You weren't there?'

'No, I came in the ambulance with you. We both did.' Carliss gestured to Nina.

Lucia was taken aback and touched at the thought that he cared enough not to leave her side.

The policeman continued. 'The DS had an easy time of it in the interview room. She confessed to both murders straightaway, not that they could get much sense out of her beyond that. Kept mumbling the same thing over and over again. I've jotted it down somewhere.' He raked furiously through his coat pockets and extracted a crumpled piece of paper, clearly ripped out of his meticulously kept book. '"Child no longer required. Does not fit in with my new position." Who would be callous enough to do that? Abandon a child like you'd return an unwanted pair of shoes?'

'You're right, and that's why Emilia killed her almost-adoptive mother,' Lucia said quietly. 'The first adoption attempt failed because the Professor, or Olga Galina, or whatever you want to call her, no longer wanted the baby. A job promotion comes along and suddenly, a child turns from a desire into a burden.'

Lucia felt her concentration waning at times, but her thought processes were as sharp as ever. At the same time, she was acutely aware of her own physical frailty. She needed to speak before the medication lulled her back into senselessness.

'I'd like to tell the whole story from the beginning, if I may, now that all the pieces finally fit together. If Emilia's had a nervous breakdown, as I suspect she would have done, it may be a while till you get any sense out of her.' Lucia fixed Carliss with a determined look and struggled to pull herself upright. She had pins and needles in her legs from having been sedentary for so long.

Nina rushed over and propped her up with a couple of pillows. She stroked her bedridden friend's hair affectionately. 'We want to hear it, Lulu. This way we can all have closure on this agonizing affair.'

Lucia proceeded in a steady, measured voice, the kind she employed when there were uncomfortable matters to present. 'To understand why Olga Galina died, we must first understand how she lived. Inevitably, I've had to fill in the gaps with my own suppositions, though I believe the principal facts to be accurate as they happened. She was born of humble stock, most likely in or around Brest, on the Soviet-Polish border, in present-day Belarus. She worked her way out of poverty, left for Minsk, went to university and made a name for herself there. A tenured position in the Faculty of Applied Mathematics at the Belarusian State University is a coveted goal. Then, one day, like many others before her, she's approached by the secret services – the Belarusian KGB, if you will. She's certainly in the right line of work – cybernetics in the former Soviet Union was, after all, the precursor to cyber warfare.'

'Impressive knowledge,' said DCI Carliss.

'I've done my basic reading, as you can see. Olga Galina is smart and ruthless, and she rises quickly through the ranks. We've all quipped about the meaning of Clytemnestra…' Lucia paused for breath and shook her head in a futile attempt to dispel the mounting pain.

'Shall I get the nurse?' the policeman fussed with concern.

'No, I'm fine. They'll only give me more painkillers, and I want to get to the end of my account before I lose the plot.' Despite the discomfort, she steeled herself to plough on. 'One day, Olga Galina takes on the job to flush out the mole at the ministry of health, who also happens to be Dr Glover's fiancée. He's spirited away back to the UK, and spends years wondering what really happened out there.'

'Why do you think she comes from a humble background?' the detective stopped her in mid-flow.

'Ah, yes. The errors in her Russian. You'll probably jump in to correct my pronunciation, Nina, but I believe it's called *trasianka*.'

'It literally means low quality hay,' Nina took over. 'In linguistic terms, it means a mixture of Belarusian and Russian spoken primarily by the lower orders. It goes to show that despite her extensive education, Olga couldn't erase all traces of her origins – at least not in the shrewd eyes of a native speaker of literary Russian such as her former colleague, Dr Ivanov.'

Lucia stroked the bedcovers absently for a few moments, then raised her head with renewed determination. 'In the midst of her life of violence and intrigue, Olga is only human. She's at the age when most women have settled down and are raising a family – you must remember this was a relatively traditional society – and she desperately hankers for a child of her own. She doesn't want a husband, nor does she want to bear children herself, which makes adoption her best bet. Sentimentality, nostalgia, call it what you like, draws her back to Brest, her place of birth. She comes across Emilia at the orphanage, and the stage is set. But then Olga gets promoted at work – perhaps unexpectedly. Maybe it's genuine, or maybe it's a ploy by the KGB to lull her into a false sense of security. Either way, I doubt we'll ever know. She might have become a liability, or it could just be pure jealousy at her success. The powers that be decide she needs to be disposed of. She gets wind of the plot against her and defects to the UK, where she swaps valuable information for a new identity and a quiet life – and Professor Alla Kiseleva is born. No wonder your MI5 contacts couldn't track her down.'

'Home Office,' the inspector swiftly intervened to correct her.

'Sorry – slip of the tongue.' Lucia's half-smile indicated she would let this one pass. 'The Professor's existence in this country is prosaic by comparison with her former life. She marries, her husband dies and leaves her a sizeable house and a nice amount of money, and she spends the rest of her career at the Collaborative Mathematical Society. Her life becomes accidentally intertwined with Adam Corcoran's – the orphaned son of her beloved friend, whom she takes in.'

'Adam's effective adoption could have been some sort of misplaced maternal instinct, to make up for Emilia's abandonment all those years ago,' said Nina.

'Is amateur psychology another one of your talents, along with speaking Russian?' joked Carliss.

'One day, the Professor, now retired, advertises for an assistant to help with her latest book.' Lucia laughed. 'My maths might be in the gutter, but even I can work out that a tome discussing Soviet versus American cybernetics smells a little fishy. On the Soviet front, she wouldn't have had access to any information worth publishing unless she was extremely well connected. Along with her creaky Russian, that's what led me to think she wasn't the person in her passport. Then Nina dug up her MI6 file, and I knew I was on the right track.'

'The words Emilia was repeating down at the station. How did she discover Olga didn't want her anymore?'

'Patience, David,' snapped back Lucia, rather more sharply than intended. It was the first time she had called the inspector by his first name since their evening together in Kentish Town. She liked the way it sounded. 'I'm coming on to that. Separately, Emilia is faced with yet another personal tragedy. Perhaps her parents told her she was adopted, perhaps they didn't. I'd venture to guess she found out while sorting through their estate after their death. She finds the doll, possibly her birth certificate, and finds out her true identity. Just like we did, she contacts the Belarusian authorities. It takes months, years even, and they finally get back to her with the records we saw for ourselves. What's to say the paperwork she got sent didn't contain the reason for the aborted adoption?'

'It wasn't in the papers we got sent,' retorted the inspector.

'Consider yourself lucky that the public functionaries of Brest deigned to send you anything at all,' said Nina. 'You know how slowly these Eastern European bureaucracies work.'

'OK, what next?' said Carliss.

'Emilia tracks down the university photo of Olga and realizes it's her employer.' There was a natural break in Lucia's monologue as she sighed with sadness. 'I feel for the poor girl. Her behaviour in the aftermath of her parents' death and the ensuing scandal has clinical depression written all over it – not being able to hold down her job, flitting around purposelessly. And, just as she thinks she's got her life back on track with the Professor, the bombshell is dropped. It would be enough to tip a more mentally stable person over the edge. So, she plots and waits. The opportunity presents itself at the impromptu tea party – given the knack for making enemies that the victim had, it's a rare event, not to be missed. There's a sufficiently large number of possible suspects, some with potential motive, some without. It's the perfect set up for Emilia to disappear in.'

'The way she did it was nothing short of masterful,' said Nina admiringly. 'So simple, yet so effective.'

'Wasn't it just.' Lucia felt she needed to expound the method again, so as to persuade herself that a human being had actually been cruel and devious enough to put it into practice. 'It was the tiny speck of plastic stuck to the rim of the Professor's champagne coupe that gave it away. A not quite perfect murder.' Lucia remembered, not without pride, how Carliss's jaw visibly dropped when she explained her theory. 'The inside of the glass was covered in transparent spray-on film, the kind you can buy in any hardware shop. It's normally used to protect the paint on cars, and it peels off in seconds without leaving any marks. I've got some in my van, which is why I thought of it. Besides, the glass was ornately decorated, so any imperfections or suspicious opacity would have been masked by the pattern. Emilia knew she only had seconds to dispose of the evidence after the Professor collapsed. To remove the glass any earlier would have risked insufficient ingestion of the poison or could have drawn unwanted attention to the item. Once the desired effect was achieved, there wouldn't have been enough time to remove the glass and wash it out, but Emilia could dab the remaining champagne with a tissue, whip the film clean off and pour a little fresh drink back in to fool the police.

Except not all the film came off. The speck must have got stuck on a portion of the rim that didn't touch the Professor's mouth. Since the rim wasn't contaminated with the 1080, forensics consequently found nothing.'

'A bold move, and prone to so many screw-ups,' remarked Carliss wryly. 'You showed me the trick – it's childishly simple if you keep calm and know what you're doing. And what about Adam? Where does he fit in?'

'Adam was collateral damage, not to mention Emilia must have hated him – the adopted child that took her place in the Professor's admittedly short-lived affections. Nina's psychological assessment is most likely correct. He was sleeping with Emilia, so sooner or later he was bound to come across something incriminating. He found the doll, and from there he dug around until he uncovered the truth. With his professional connections, he must have been in the perfect position to pull plenty of strings to get access to the incriminating paperwork. He may have even confronted Emilia. He must have deduced she had a very strong motive for the Professor's murder, which is why Emilia had to get rid of him. The fact that he was a cocaine addict made it ridiculously easy. She had kept back some poison, just in case, which she now deployed. It was an even more audacious move than the Professor's murder, as Emilia could have been a prime suspect, but by then she was desperate and running out of time. On the other hand, you could say she hedged her bets. She had worked out that the police had Adam down as the Professor's killer, so guilt-induced suicide fitted the bill. He was a known drug user, after all.'

'What escapes me, Lulu, is how she messed up and left foundation on the inside of the tin,' asked Nina.

Lucia recalled the glitch. 'The foundation tube was cracked. She must have kept in her bag the disposable gloves that she used to open the tin. A little foundation got smeared on the gloves, which in turn was transferred to the inside of the tin as she reached to collect the poison. Another small, but this time fatal error.'

'And Glover?' the inspector asked curiously.

'I would venture to say that he and Emilia seem closer than first impressions would suggest. For all we know, Emilia could have confided in him when she found out about the Professor's real past. What's to say that the connection to Belarus didn't bring back the memory of his fiancée's death? It can't have come as a surprise that the maths faculty in Minsk was a hotbed of KGB spies. Then he remembers the brooch, and suddenly it all falls into place.'

'The Professor died as she lived – malicious, scheming, self-obsessed,' concluded DCI Carliss. 'She seemed to leave a trail of destruction wherever she went.'

Aside from Adam, cut out of Professor Kiseleva's life on a selfish whim, just like Emilia had been, Lucia also thought of John Walker, the blackmailed barrister, and of Mrs Byrne, the long-suffering housekeeper.

'How did you know it wasn't Glover?' said the policeman.

Lucia smiled victoriously, even though she had exhausted her last reserves of energy. 'His stiff fingers you mentioned after you met with him at his surgery. Most likely arthritis. He can't have easily got the poison out of the tin – it was quite an effort to open that lid, as I now know for myself – nor spray the film on the coupe and remove it fast enough for nobody to notice.'

'You've done enough. You need to rest, Lulu,' decreed Nina as she signalled to Carliss that they should leave their friend in peace.

Chapter 35

Saturday, 17th October (six weeks after the murder)

The weather forecast of an Indian summer over the weekend had been received with universal disbelief. Cafes and restaurants opened their doors cautiously, not daring to populate the pavement with tables and chairs lest the unyielding rain they had endured over the past week wouldn't subside. As the sun rose at seven seventeen, it became apparent that the prediction might hold after all.

Lucia pushed up the sash window and breathed in the damp but unmistakably warming morning air. Hampstead High Street was just starting to wake up. The establishment across the road was already doing a roaring trade in freshly baked baguettes and countless varieties of milky coffee. She had just recently finished the course of painkillers that the hospital had sent her home with. Aside from the occasional dizzy spell and largely ignored instructions to cut down on caffeine and alcohol, she was back to normal.

The time she had spent recuperating in the comfort of the Chanlers' Belgravia home had been the equivalent of a no expenses spared holiday. The butler and the housekeeper had waited on her hand and foot, and Nina had barely left her side as they read, talked, and remembered. Without the aid of illicit chemicals or drink, Lucia finally slept with the wantonness of a small child, as if the concussion had reset her brain. She would have been unlikely to reclaim her freedom and go home had it not been for an unexpected phone call from Mrs Byrne.

'Hello, Lucia.'

'Mrs Byrne.' The Irish lilt rang like an alien language in her ears. She hadn't recognized the number of the Beatrice Hall landline.

'How are you, child? I heard they let you leave hospital.' The voice was tinged with genuine concern, but there was something else at play, as if a fog had lifted.

'Better, thank you.' Lucia surmised the police, and by implication Detective Chief Inspector Carliss, would have been in and out of the Hall. Emilia had been arrested and duly charged with the murders of Olga Galina, also known as Professor Alla Kiseleva, and Adam Corcoran.

'Oh, I'm so glad to hear it. It's like the world has suddenly turned upside down. Emilia, of all people…' The horrified shudder at the housekeeper's end of the line was palpable. 'What the Professor did to her… I'm sorry, I know I shouldn't speak ill of the dead. It's a heartless thing to say, but I can't help thinking Alla Kiseleva got what she deserved.'

It hadn't taken long for the papers to get wind of the sensational affair – not just the red tops, but even the customarily serious publications couldn't get enough of the sordid details. The irresistible combination of drugs, death, false identities and a Cold War spy caper made for journalism of minimum efforts and maximum returns.

Mrs Byrne continued with an invigorated tone. 'I didn't know whether you'd heard, so I thought I'd give you a ring myself. That Society's inherited the house, and they want to keep me on as a caretaker.'

So that was the source of the audible spring in her step, thought Lucia.

The housekeeper wittered on. 'I said yes straightaway, of course. I was dreading having to leave and fend for myself, after all these years. The place might look like a museum, but it's my home. The thing is, they've put me in charge of the place, and they want the redecorating to resume. I thought, well… depending on how your recovery is going… that you might want your old job back. Thought I'd give you first dibs, in any case.'

It couldn't have come at a better time. Before breathlessly accepting, Lucia paused to wonder at the discovery. 'How did the house end up in the hands of the Collaborative Mathematical Society, Mrs Byrne?'

'Adam left it to them in his will.' The voice was lowered furtively, even though there wouldn't have been anyone to eavesdrop. 'I'm not really supposed to know this, but the solicitor was here the other day – nice man, that Mr Platt, and the baby's thriving, from what I hear – gathering papers and whatnot, and he let it slip, you see. When Adam was appointed executor of the Professor's will, she said she would only leave him Beatrice Hall if he in turn made a will leaving it to the Society. He hardly had much choice in the matter, did he? They're looking to turn it into a new library, they said. They would have liked to name it after the Professor, but, given the circumstances, they thought it might be a tad… inappropriate. Either way, here I am, with a roof over my head.'

Mrs Byrne sounded like she was suddenly years younger. Lucia was pleased for her. It provided some degree of equitable reparation for the housekeeper's unenviable existence.

'I'd be delighted to carry on with the work. Thank you for thinking of me,' Lucia replied. She needed to jumpstart her life – the torpor she had been forced into was making her itch with boredom. She would start first thing on Monday. The prospect of returning to Beatrice Hall with no portentous events hanging over her head was cause for joy. At last, the place was truly her own canvas, to craft into whatever she chose. The project would be her masterpiece, and with the last lick of smooth paint the grisly memories would be gone.

Chapter 36

The unseasonable weather had continued past the weekend, with nothing but blue skies. Bathed in the bright sunrise, the menacing turrets of Beatrice Hall were tamed, as if bent under the unrelenting whip of a higher entity. The van zig-zagged to a familiar spot, and Lucia marvelled at the temporary stillness – far from her to be superstitious, but she couldn't shake off the feeling that the house had been released from an evil spell. She heard steps approaching the outer gate and involuntarily readied herself. Mrs Byrne kissed her fondly on the cheek like a long-lost relative.

'Come in, Lucia. It's so good you're here.' The housekeeper was changed – something in her demeanour, a sureness that hadn't been there before. The house was hers to rule as she pleased, but it wasn't arrogance or entitlement – it was the knowledge of being settled. She wore a blue Liberty patterned dress, tightly cinched at the waist, and strands of her hair still glistening with the remnants of the old auburn shade fell softly on the shoulders. She looked younger, prettier, more like the photo Lucia had glimpsed in her room.

Inside, Lucia worked until she could no longer bear the stifling heat that permeated the fabric of the building despite the open windows. She went downstairs for a break and found that most of the garden was mercifully sheltered from the sun. She could hear Margaret's voice on the other side of the fence. The only plausible explanation for the continued clattering and scraping was that they were having work done to the house. Lucia decided to investigate.

'Margaret, hi,' she shouted over the fence.

'Oh, hi, Lucia. Sorry for the noise. The removal people are here, and it's total pandemonium. Come round the front.'

Intrigued, Lucia did as she was told. The bay outside the Walkers' front door was occupied by a lorry that was methodically swallowing up their worldly possessions. Margaret stood in the doorway, hair tied up, apron on, issuing instructions.

'You're leaving?' exclaimed Lucia. Clearly, Beatrice Hall wasn't the only place in the neighbourhood where major change was underfoot.

Margaret grinned with tired eyes. 'Yes, moving on to bigger and better things. Or at least out of here. Come in, Lucia. I'll tell you all about it over a cuppa.'

The kitchen chairs had already been packed up, so they sat, somewhat awkwardly, on the floor. There was nothing left of the Walkers' home, as the off-white walls waited patiently for another family's life.

'I meant to call, but… well, you can see for yourself.' Margaret smiled wearily. 'After the horrors next door… I heard you weren't well.' Her voice trailed off, as if she had forgotten how to make small talk. 'But you're better now?'

'Don't worry, I'm fine. It's all behind us now. What's happening with you?' Lucia saw that the other woman wanted to talk, and she definitely wanted to listen.

Margaret's brown eyes narrowed as if to suppress a tear, but nothing came out. She ran her fingers through her ponytail and began. 'John was having an affair. I've known for quite some time. I might look like a trophy wife, but I didn't leave my brain at the door when I quit my job to be the good little woman.' She said this matter-of-factly, with no bitterness attached. 'He couldn't just jump the clerk or his pupil, like everyone else. It had to be bloody Frieda Alexander.'

Margaret stopped, on the verge of explaining, when Lucia cut in. 'I know who she is.' She debated for a split second whether to go further and opted for partial honesty. 'The police got wind of the affair. They also knew the Professor was blackmailing your husband. It put him on their list of suspects. I'm sorry, this is awful, but you deserve to know.'

Margaret pursed her lips and nodded in acquiescence – it obviously wasn't news to her. 'Once he knew the police was on to him, John told me everything. Shame that he couldn't keep it in his pants – two careers down the pan, and for what?' The sigh was not one of despair, but rather of dogged determination. 'I'm not walking away. He's not a bad man, just monumentally stupid, and I owe it to the children.'

'What are you going to do next?' asked Lucia. She wondered what it was that Margaret did before she became a housewife.

'We're moving to the States. South Carolina, to be precise. I always fancied living in Charleston. I've got a job offer, and the visas are already in the pipeline.' Margaret's eyes lit up, and she laughed with unbridled delight. 'After all these years, the tables have finally turned. He'll have to be the stay-at-home husband and start from scratch before he can make something of himself. A fitting punishment, I think.'

'It's quite the fall from grace. And what's your line of work, Margaret?'

'Forensic accountant. In fact, it turns out Adam worked at my old firm. He was long after my time – our paths didn't cross then. It's a small world, eh?'

Small world indeed, pondered Lucia. Very occasionally, coincidences did just happen. She marvelled at the change in Margaret – under the misleading shell of vacuity hid an intelligent and tenacious woman. 'Listen, if you need a hand when you get there – anything at all – I've got a good friend who hails from Charleston. They'd be more than happy to help.' Lucia was sure the Chanlers would go out of their way to give a leg-up to someone in need.

'Thanks, Lucia. I could do with support, that's for sure.'

Chapter 37

Later that day, standing in front of her bedroom mirror, Lucia was faced with a pleasant existential dilemma. Nina had planned an evening at the Savoy to celebrate the successful conclusion of the double murder investigation. 'And David will be there, of course – if that's what will tempt you out of your den, Lulu.' Lucia was amused that Nina and the inspector were newly on first-name terms.

Lucia was tempted, except that she didn't know what to wear. She settled for a black silk jumpsuit which, like the rest of her minimal wardrobe, walked the fine line between demure and beguiling. Sat in the taxi, she watched the darkening city whizz past and savoured the anticipation.

They were waiting for her, ensconced in one of the histrionic gold-leaf alcoves of the Beaufort Bar. It had always been Nina's favoured watering hole, so much that she emulated it in her own home. It was the detective's first visit, and he had scanned the place incredulously as he followed Nina to the best table in the house. The waiting staff acknowledged her presence with a bow of the head – she was a good customer.

When Lucia arrived, the drinks had already been ordered, a crisply cold vodka martini as her placeholder.

The blue eyes narrowed and crinkled into a broad smile. Carliss had made a special effort for the occasion. She could smell the freshly polished leather brogues, and his well-cut blazer was beyond reproach. Nina had helpfully taken the lacquered armchair, leaving Lucia no option but to sink into the black and gold patterned sofa alongside the policeman.

'Looking good, Detective.' She rested her fingers on the elegant glass. It was a million miles away from broken lives, convoluted motives, and the resulting dead bodies.

'So are you. I've done very well for myself tonight, haven't I?' He smiled at Nina, who shimmered in a pink metallic minidress that only she would have dared to wear so cavalierly. His eyes lingered on Lucia. They made a striking trio.

'Cheers. To our victory. First martinis, then champagne with dinner, then… who knows?' rejoiced Nina. She was in her element, with her blonde curls catching the low, theatrical light that reflected off her hazel eye, like a cat in the dark. Lucia wouldn't have been surprised if they'd named a cocktail after her.

Lucia took a long sip and leaned back, as if resting in an ancient Egyptian sarcophagus. All the other times that she and Nina had been here, they had drunk at the bar on the old cabaret stage, blinded by the mirrors and the possibilities. The alcoves were for lovers, or secretive businessmen striking opaque deals. Her mind wandered. She was loath to bring up the unpleasant subject of the murders but knew she couldn't find peace until she did. 'I wonder what gave Emilia the idea of the 1080.'

'Oh, Lulu, just leave it be,' Nina groaned. 'We're here to forget.'

'She probably just found it under the sink by accident, and that gave her the perfect means of killing the Professor,' Carliss said, stifling a bored yawn.

Lucia stubbornly ignored the signals that her friends weren't in the mood for talking shop. 'Perhaps. Someone whose job is to kill could have put the idea in her head.'

'Who? Glover? We can't prove it, and she confessed,' interrupted Nina impatiently.

'What do you think he got up to in Belarus? People like him have extensive knowledge of poison. And the Professor's murder was so audacious. The poison was in plain sight – anyone could have done it. You just had to keep your cool and nobody could prove it was you. And the clingfilm – that was very smart. He couldn't have done it himself – not with those stiff fingers. But, in the end, Emilia couldn't quite deliver – she made two tiny errors. She must really love him to go to prison for him. No man is worth giving up your freedom for.'

'Lucia, that's fanciful. I'm with our dear inspector on this – let bygones be bygones. You're making this story into more than it actually is,' chided Nina as she ordered another round of drinks.

Lucia wasn't wholly convinced, but she decided to let it go for the time being. All that hanging around the Professor's library pretending to sort out her papers – what was to say Emilia and Glover weren't making sure that no incriminating evidence had been left behind? Nevertheless, Emilia had owned up to her transgressions with full knowledge of the consequences, as was her prerogative. Right now, there was another matter that she wanted to set straight. 'What happened with Danny in the end?'

'We charged him. Given how much coke he had in the van, he's in a lot of trouble,' replied Carliss, sipping his fresh martini.

'And the pub?' It was Leila and Becky that Lucia was worried about.

'Not enough evidence to close it down. In all likelihood, that's where he was selling his wares, but none of his suspected customers would talk, and we found nothing. We questioned the landlady – that was an experience that nobody at the station is likely to forget any time soon – and that young barmaid, but they seemed innocent enough, at least for the record.'

Lucia had her own suspicions but decided to keep them close to her chest. Becky was probably not in on it – for all her airs, she was surprisingly naïve. Recalling Leila's erratic behaviour, Lucia had surmised that the landlady was turning a blind eye to Danny's line of work in exchange for a steady supply of the product. You couldn't hold it against her – one of the more plausible stories about the woman's escape involved a high price paid to the guards on the Turkish border, the kind that didn't involve any money.

The detective's eyes were on Lucia, weighing her up. 'What would you have to say about joining the police as a civilian investigator?' He watched and waited for her reaction.

This really had come out of the blue. Lucia was speechless. Nina too was watching her closely.

'Well? I hadn't banked on total silence,' the inspector said.

'I don't know. I need to think about it. It's a tempting idea, I must admit.' The grin on Lucia's face said it all. 'Is that actually a thing? Don't you need… qualifications?' It sounded too good to be true.

'Yes and no. You need investigative experience, and I'd say you've got plenty. Worth a shot, in any case, if you're up for it,' replied Carliss, as if he dared her to refuse.

Martinis morphed into a lavish dinner, and they found plenty to talk about that wasn't murder. Hours later, after all the champagne had been drunk, Nina kissed them both goodbye and ordered a taxi. 'Good night, darlings. I know when I'm a third wheel so I'm off. I've just remembered I've got a husband.'

Lucia rested her arm on the back of the sofa and beckoned to the waiter for the cocktail list. For tonight at least, all was good with the world.

List of Characters

Lucia Steer – heroine, interior designer and former lawyer

DCI David Carliss – Senior Investigating Officer, Metropolitan Police

Professor Alla Kiseleva – victim

Adam Corcoran – Professor's nephew

Dr Edmund Glover – Professor's GP

Emilia Poole – Professor's assistant

Orla Byrne – Professor's housekeeper

John Walker – barrister, Professor's neighbour

Margaret Walker – John's wife

Frieda Alexander – judge, John's lover

Nina Chanler, née Lexington – Lucia's best friend

Walter Chanler – Nina's husband

Virginia Lexington – Nina's mother

Danny Garrett – builder, Lucia's competitor

Jimbo – Danny's apprentice

Dr Oleg Ivanov – Professor's former colleague

Herbert Jennings – caretaker at the Collaborative Mathematical Society

Gemma – receptionist at Runciman Parry

Becky – bar tender at the Red Lion

Leila – publican at the Red Lion

Julius Platt – Professor's solicitor

PC George Harding – Metropolitan Police officer

If you enjoyed this book, please let others know by leaving a quick review on Amazon. Also, if you spot anything untoward in the paperback, get in touch. We strive for the best quality and appreciate reader feedback.

editor@thebookfolks.com

More in this series

MURDER ON THE HEATH (book 2)

Now working as a civilian investigator helping out DCI Carliss and Kentish Town CID, Lucia is proving invaluable whilst inevitably ruffling a few feathers along the way.

When a relationship coach is found dead, apparently electrocuted by a coffee maker, Lucia makes short work of a killer's attempt to hide a murder. But finding out who was so ready to kill in cold blood will take some doing.

Other titles of interest:

THE ALLEY by Kathy Garthwaite

A gunshot rings out through a small Vancouver Island town. A man is dead in the jewelry store. Detective Marlowe Flint must work out if it was a robbery gone wrong, or an organized hit. But witnesses are reluctant to come forward, and when another man is beaten to within an inch of his life, the killer may slip through the detective's grasp.

DEAD PRETTY by Candy Denman

When a woman is found dead in Hastings, Sussex, the medical examiner feels a murder has taken place. Yet she feels the police are not doing enough because the victim is a prostitute. Dr Callie Hughes will conduct her own investigation, no matter the danger.

Printed in Great Britain
by Amazon

66854613R00135